Map of the town of THEDGEROOT
by S.S. Meriwether

dirt road

The Factory

drainage ditch

Blackhope Creek

drain tunnel

Blackhope Pond

ant trap

trail

cows

collapsed tunnel

more cows

Thedgeroot Middle School

to other, better places

sheep for a change

Legend:
- highway
- mine shaft entrance
- mine tunnel
- street
- fields
- fence
- dirt road
- building
- woods

better places this way also

THE HAUNTED SERPENT

Dora M. Mitchell

STERLING CHILDREN'S BOOKS
New York

To Grandma Margaret and
Grandma Dorie. I miss you.

STERLING CHILDREN'S BOOKS
New York

An Imprint of Sterling Publishing Co., Inc.
1166 Avenue of the Americas
New York, NY 10036

ISBN 978-1-4549-2785-3

Distributed in Canada by Sterling Publishing Co., Inc.
c/o Canadian Manda Group, 664 Annette Street
Toronto, Ontario M6S 2C8, Canada
Distributed in the United Kingdom by GMC Distribution Services
Castle Place, 166 High Street, Lewes, East Sussex BN7 1XU, England
Distributed in Australia by NewSouth Books
45 Beach Street, Coogee, NSW 2034, Australia

For information about custom editions, special sales, and premium
and corporate purchases, please contact Sterling Special Sales at 800-805-5489
or specialsales@sterlingpublishing.com.

Manufactured in the United States of America

Lot #:
2   4   6   8   10   9   7   5   3   1
05/18

www.sterlingpublishing.com

Cover and interior design by Heather Kelly

Chapter One

Note to Self: Stop Going in Woods Alone

From the Research Notebook of S.S. Meriwether

Even before he saw the dead guy, Spaulding Meriwether was in a bad mood. His feet were wet, his hands were freezing, and he was all alone in the middle of a dark, foggy forest.

Worst of all, he was feeling like an idiot. He knew what he was getting into when he came out here. He'd heard kids at school saying there was strange stuff going on in the woods outside town, stuff that sounded to him like it could be part of some kind of creepy secret ritual. So what did he do when he heard all this? Stay far away, like any sensible person? Oh no, not S. S. Meriwether—he had to go investigate.

Clouds of fat, black flies buzzed up from the grass everywhere he stepped—unusual for late October. Before him, Blackhope Pond lay dark and silent, like an enormous, lidless eye. If anything strange had been going on out here, there was no sign of it now. No burned-out bonfires, no pentacles scratched in the dirt, no candle stubs or broomsticks or whatever people actually used for occult rituals.

He glanced back at the pond. Then again, anything could be hiding in that inky-black water and he wouldn't have the least idea. The woods were so thick, every murderer and bear and swamp thing in the neighborhood could be lurking in there and he'd never know.

So when he spotted the dead guy a few yards away, he wasn't exactly surprised—it only confirmed how dumb he was. He knew something dangerous was going on. For once, he'd rather not have been right.

Okay, so maybe it was kind of a leap to assume the man was dead. Especially considering he was standing upright and everything. He was even wearing a suit, gloves, and a rather dapper hat. Just because his suit was ragged and covered with suspicious brown stains, and on second glance the hat was all squashed and lopsided, and his skin was chalky-white and sort of squishy-looking, it didn't officially mean he was dead. Still, this guy was the closest thing to evidence Spaulding had found, so he slid his research notebook out of his back pocket and jotted a quick note. When he got home, he'd add a sketch of the scene while it was fresh in his mind. Spaulding was very thorough about his research notes.

Anyway, even if the guy wasn't dead, there was something funny about wandering the woods in formal attire. Spaulding didn't want to stick around to find out what he was up to.

4:58 pm—Dead guy* lurking by Blackhope Pond?
*Note: may not** have been dead.
**In fact, unlikely to have been dead,
statistically speaking.

Very slowly, he backed away, placing his feet carefully so he wouldn't make a sound. He took several steps without so much as snapping a twig. Then the harsh jangle of his cell phone shattered the silence.

The man's head jerked up. His hat cast a deep shadow over most of his face, but it almost looked like there was something *moving* on his neck and jaw—small, white, wriggly somethings—

Spaulding pushed the thought away. Now was not the time to let his imagination get out of control.

He grabbed his phone and fumbled to turn it off . . . but it was already off. "Weird," he muttered as he stuffed the phone back in his pocket to deal with later. A moody cell phone wasn't exactly tops on the priority list just now.

The man took a step closer. His face was turned in Spaulding's direction, but there was still a screen of trees between them—it was possible he hadn't spotted Spaulding yet. Spaulding headed for his bike as quickly as he could without quite breaking into a run. Behind him, footsteps crunched slowly through the leaves.

Just how far away had he left his bike, anyway? It seemed like it was taking forever to get back to it. He squinted ahead. There it was, lying near some twisted old tree stumps on the other side of the dirt road that dead-ended at the edge of the pond.

He started running, his footsteps squelching as he crossed the rutted road. Reaching his bike at last, he hauled it upright, his heart pounding. He turned back toward the road, ready to hop on and go. Only now the man in the suit was standing in the middle of the road. Spaulding would have to pass within arms' reach of him to get away.

Spaulding swallowed hard. His knees were quivering too much to swing his leg over his bike. His foot caught on the seat, and his bike clattered to the ground. "*Gah!*"

He gave up on getting his shaky legs to cooperate with mounting his bike and just *ran*, wheeling the bike alongside. Maybe if he ran past at top speed and kept the bike between them . . .

The man seemed confused. He still wasn't looking directly at Spaulding, and his head swung slowly from side to side like a dog casting for a scent. But then he suddenly snapped around to face Spaulding fully. There was something off about his movements—they were stiff yet fast, like a badly animated cartoon. And now that he was closer, Spaulding could hear the humming of the cloud of flies that surrounded him.

In a burst of adrenaline, he jumped onto his bike at a run. His feet hit the pedals, and he tore down the road.

As he whizzed by, the man lunged toward him. Spaulding swerved wildly and felt an outstretched hand graze his back. He flattened himself over the handlebars. Sharp fingernails scratched at his sweatshirt but didn't catch hold.

He rounded a curve in the road. Not far ahead, the smooth asphalt of the highway gleamed. He'd be able to pick up speed once he was on the pavement, if he made it that far.

From the corner of his eye, Spaulding saw the man in the suit leap forward again. A dank smell washed over him, like rotten things in stagnant water. Something heavy hit the spokes of his back tire with a loud twang. The bike lurched—

The tire was stuck.

He was falling. The man had to be right behind him now. Any second, he would feel cold, damp fingers latch on—

But somehow he kept himself upright. With one great, tearing effort, he ripped his wheel free of whatever had tangled in the spokes and took off again. His tires gripped the highway and he skidded through the turn. Whoever—or *whatever*—the man in the suit was, he couldn't keep up with Spaulding now.

The footsteps slowed and then faded away. When he risked a glance back, the road was empty. He caught a flash of movement in the trees and just saw the man disappearing down a narrow, muddy trail that led into the woods.

He didn't want to stop until he got back to the safety of town, and maybe not even then. But there was still something hung up in the spokes—he could hear it catching with every turn of the wheels. Reluctantly, he steered over to the side of the road and dismounted.

An unrecognizable clump was stuck in the metal wires—something damp and stringy. Gingerly, he picked at the tangle until the mass came away in his hand.

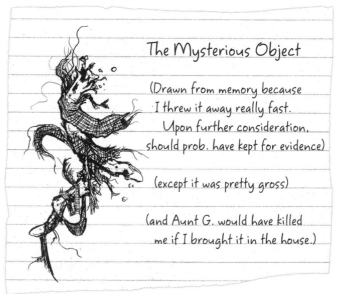

The Mysterious Object

(Drawn from memory because
I threw it away really fast.
Upon further consideration,
should prob. have kept for evidence)

(except it was pretty gross)

(and Aunt G. would have killed
me if I brought it in the house.)

Shreds of rotten fabric fell away from a cluster of small, splintered bones and sinew. Maybe it was some kind of totem, or someone's horrible idea of jewelry. But mostly, it looked like . . . *fingers.*

When Spaulding got home, the house was dark and quiet. That wasn't a surprise—his great-aunt Gwendolyn was always in her study working at this time of day. Still, he felt a twinge of disappointment. He wasn't exactly in the mood to be alone.

He chewed his lip and looked at the closed study door. He wasn't technically supposed to disturb her when she was working. But he did have a good excuse; he could ask her why she'd called earlier. He tapped on the door and peered in.

Aunt Gwen didn't look up from her laptop. Her gray hair was falling out of a bun held with a pen and a pencil, her heavy black-framed glasses were sliding down her nose, and her sweater was buttoned wrong. "Right in the middle of a scene, Spaulding—can it wait?" she asked, not bothering with a greeting.

"Sorry. I was just wondering why you called." He held up his cell phone and waggled it at her.

She yanked the pen free from her bun, which slid further down the side of her head. "Wasn't me, pet," she said as she scribbled a note on the stack of papers beside her. "Probably someone from school, right? One of your new friends? Run along now, I'll catch up with you at dinner."

Spaulding frowned. Nobody at school had his number.

Nobody at school knew his *name*, practically. He shut the study door and headed upstairs, scrolling through the call logs on his ancient flip-phone. Aunt Gwen was right—there was no missed call from her. There was no record of a call from anyone.

In his room, Spaulding pulled out his favorite paranormal encyclopedia and flipped through the dog-eared pages until he found the entry he was looking for:

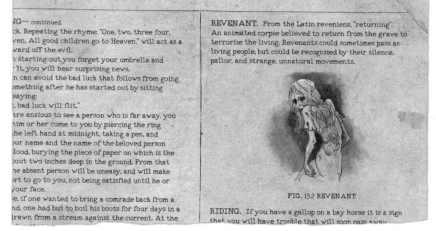

ENCYCLOPEDIA OF FOLKLORE AND SUPERSTITION   662

JG-- continued.
ck. Repeating the rhyme: "One, two, three four, ven, All good children go to Heaven," will act as a ward off the evil.
1 starting out you forget your umbrella and · it, you will hear surprising news.
n can avoid the bad luck that follows from going omething after he has started out by sitting saying:
;, bad luck will flit."
are anxious to see a person who is far away, you aim or her come to you by piercing the ring .he left hand at midnight, taking a pen, and our name and the name of the beloved person lood, burying the piece of paper on which is the pout two inches deep in the ground. From that ne absent person will be uneasy, and will make art to go to you, not being satisfied until he or your face.
ie, if one wanted to bring a comrade back from a nd, one had but to boil his boots for four days in a rawn from a stream against the current. At the

REVENANT. From the Latin *reveniens*, "returning". An animated corpse believed to return from the grave to terrorize the living. Revenants could sometimes pass as living people, but could be recognized by their silence, pallor, and strange, unnatural movements.

FIG. 152 REVENANT

RIDING. If you have a gallop on a bay horse it is a sign that you will have trouble that will soon pass away.

He slammed the book shut.

He was going crazy.

After all, what had he really seen? Just a pale, smelly, dirty person wearing a squashed hat. With some flies and bugs on him. And yeah, he'd acted a little *unusual*, but it was a pretty big leap from there to *Night of the Living Dead*.

He was probably just some poor homeless guy living out in the woods. Maybe he'd wanted to chase Spaulding away from where he was camping. Maybe he hadn't *chased* him at all. What if he'd just been heading in the same direction, aiming for that trail? When Spaulding tore past on his bike like a lunatic, he'd probably just knocked the guy off balance.

But then there was the Mysterious Object. Where had the fingers come from, if not the man in the suit?

The answer was, they *weren't* fingers, obviously. They'd sure *looked* like fingers. But they weren't.

Anyway, even if the dead were waking, he'd just have to focus on the bright side: this would make an excellent story to tell the kids at school.

Chapter Two

Note to Self:
Also Stop Going to Homeroom

Spaulding awoke with a cold knot of dread in the pit of his stomach. He couldn't remember exactly what he'd been dreaming about, but the vague pictures that appeared when he shut his eyes were full of insects and dead things.

Ol' Weird Joe

Wears scarf, earmuffs, & short-shorts in all weather conditions.

Stench radius approx. 15 ft.

Believes secret Moon government is spying on him.

He walked to the bus stop slowly—it took a long time to peek around every corner and behind every tree. He didn't spot anyone who appeared undead (except some of the more peculiar townsfolk, who always looked that way), but he did manage to take so long that he almost missed the bus and had to run the last two blocks.

By the time he got to the bus stop, he was sweaty, out of breath, and his hair was all floppy like he hated. To top it off, he skidded in the gravel on the corner and nearly fell on his face.

Marietta Bellwood, who lived down the street, sneered at his undignified arrival, then went back to pretending he was invisible. She had been doing that ever since the day he moved into the neighborhood, when he'd gone door-to-door formally introducing himself. He still didn't know what had gone wrong. He'd even planned his introduction ahead of time to be sure it would convey a tone of casual sophistication.

"Meriwether—S.S. Meriwether," he'd said, in a casually sophisticated sort of way, sticking his hand out at her. "But my friends call me Boat." (This was a lie, but he was determined to establish a nickname for himself right away, before anyone had a chance to come up with something uncool. Like "Spudling," for example, his accursed family nickname.)

Marietta had stared at him like he was made of spiders. Then she'd begun ignoring him, which it seemed she planned to continue doing for the rest of their lives.

Perhaps the introduction had been a miscalculation.

Spaulding climbed the bus steps and slumped into a seat. As

Marietta Bellwood

· Fellow sixth grader.

· Seems to be one of the "cool kids."

· Unwilling to explain how one gets to be "cool."

always, no one took the seat next to him. The bus rumbled away from the curb, and he turned to the window to distract himself.

The scenery didn't do much to cheer him up. Thedgeroot was an old town, and most of the buildings looked like they hadn't been painted or modernized since its California Gold Rush heyday. Many of the shops and houses were empty, their windows either boarded up or shuttered, as if to stop anything from getting in—or out.

Pull it together, Boat, Spaulding thought. (Yeah, the new nickname was aces.)

But just then, the bus passed the road to Blackhope Pond.

What if the man in the suit was lurking in the trees again? What if he was out there searching for his lost fingers? (Only they weren't fingers.)

Spaulding kept his eyes glued to the turnoff as it flashed by. There was no one there. As he'd expected, of course. He folded his arms and pretended he hadn't really been looking at all.

A mile or two farther on, the bus passed a barren field encircled by a chain link fence. In the middle of the field stood a cluster of industrial buildings and towering silos. The gates were chained shut. The windows gaped, the glass broken and jagged like sharp teeth in cavernous mouths. The whole place appeared long abandoned, except for a thread of white vapor that trailed from the smokestacks and bled away into the fog.

Spaulding craned his neck at the sign as they drove by, puzzling over the strange slogan for the hundredth time:

Every time he rode the bus, he wondered about that place. He tried to imagine the factory back when the town was young: full of people bustling around, busily *imagining* and *innovatising*—whatever that meant. What had they made there in the old days? And why would the chimneys be smoking now, when everything else about the place looked so forlorn and empty?

He glanced around to ask one of the other kids, but couldn't catch anyone's eye. Marietta was looking over at him, but she whipped a book up in front of her face as soon as he opened his mouth.

He sighed and reached for his notebook again—the *Notes to Self* were really piling up lately.

When the bus pulled up at school, he brightened. If

anything could get his mind off his worries, it was school. He'd only started public school a few weeks ago, and it was still new and exciting. Up till now, he and Aunt Gwen had moved so often that it had been easier for him to be home-schooled. But this time she intended to stay put for a while, or so she said, back in the town where she'd grown up. Spaulding figured it was the perfect time to try regular school and make some friends his age, which wasn't something he'd really done before. His friends had tended to be Aunt Gwen's writer buddies, or four-legged, or . . . well, that was pretty much it.

That was all going to change now. School hadn't been quite as great as he'd imagined so far, but it was bound to get better soon.

Thedgeroot Middle School does not make enthusiasm easy to maintain.

He made his way to his homeroom, doing his best to ignore the cracked bricks and peeling paint all over the building.

"Ah, Spaulding, my *leetle Schnuckiputzi!*"

As he walked into class, Mrs. Welliphaunt, his homeroom teacher, greeted him in her cracked, faintly accented voice. She wore her usual old-fashioned dress with a high collar and long sleeves.

"Come up here, my dear. Let Mrs. Welliphaunt have a look at you. You look tired, no? You do not sleep well?"

Hesitantly, Spaulding approached her desk. Mrs. Welliphaunt meant well, he supposed, but she also seemed a little . . . *insane*. She made him nervous.

"I'm fine, ma'am. I—"

Before he could say more, her thin, papery hands shot out and caught his wrist in a tight grip. She pulled him closer, her pale eyes boring into his. Then she flipped his hand over and squinted at his palm, tracing the lines and muttering to herself about signs and dark portents. It was better than having her glaring into his eyes, but only by a little.

Seconds passed. She didn't seem to be planning on letting go of his wrist. Ever.

Mrs. Welliphaunt

Bizarrely old-fashioned clothing

Unnaturally happy for a teacher

"World's Best Teacher" mug she definitely bought for herself

"Um, thanks, Mrs. Welliphaunt. I guess I'll just . . . go . . . sit . . ." He gave his hand a small, polite tug. She ignored it, still fixated on his palm.

"Short life-line," she whispered to herself. "Not surprising for a troublemaker, though . . ."

He gave up on being polite and flat-out wrenched himself free. The old woman's hands remained outstretched for a moment, then slowly sank to her lap. She watched him back nervously to his desk.

Well, that was *awkward*. He wiped his hands on his pants surreptitiously. But that was old ladies for you—always with the cheek-pinching, and the dimple-admiring, and the holding-your-hands-in-a-powerful-grip-while-making-grim-predictions . . .

He wiped his hands some more.

You can't go around getting scared by every little old lady who's a tiny bit overly friendly, he told himself sternly as he took his seat. In the future, he'd simply make sure not to get within arm's reach of her.

※ ※ ※

A short time later, Spaulding sat in his first-period classroom. So far, he thought, his first few weeks of public school had been highly educational. Just not necessarily in an information-from-a-textbook kind of way.

What I Have Learned So Far

Contributing to class discussions = teasing.

Freely expressing opinions = teasing.

Dressing up for assemblies
(a perfectly appropriate time to look one's best) = teasing.

And dealing with the teachers wasn't much easier than the students. Spaulding's teacher for first period, Mr. Robards, was a perfect example. Mr. Robards taught history. Spaulding *loved* history. And yet Mr. Robards hardly seemed to appreciate his enthusiasm.

At the moment, Mr. Robards was droning on about the California Gold Rush and doing his best to suck the life out of a subject that should have been exciting. Spaulding, for one, was thrilled to learn that the countryside around Thedgeroot was riddled with abandoned mines. The other students were not exactly enthralled.

"Besides the mineshafts, tailings ponds, and other radical reshaping of the land itself," Mr. Robards said over the sound of mass yawning, "there is another legacy of mining in our county. I am referring, of course, to the toxins in our water system. These toxins include mercury and arsenic, and the effects of this contamination are still—all right, all *right*! What *is* it, Mr. Meriwether?"

Spaulding stopped frantically waving his hand. "Are we going to talk about red mercury, Mr. Robards?" he asked. "I've always found it fascinating."

A few desks over, Katrina Waverly, the most popular girl in the sixth grade, gave a loud snort. Katrina was in most of his classes, and besides him, she was the only kid who ever voluntarily answered questions. She'd even answered some stuff *he* didn't know.

"Red mercury is folklore, not history," Katrina said.

Spaulding leaned over his desk to see her. "You've heard of it? Most people haven't."

She sniffed and tossed her long, brown hair over her shoulder. "Duh."

"Well, anyway," he said, turning back to Mr. Robards, "not everyone thinks it's folk-

Katrina Waverly—
Ruler of the sixth grade.

Make good impression on K. =
shortcut to acquiring friends??

lore. And folklore is an aspect of history. And it's interesting."

Mr. Robards pinched the bridge of his nose. "Very well, Mr. Meriwether. Red mercury is an imaginary substance, which is imagined to be created in some sort of mysterious alchemical process from real mercury—the toxic chemical we are actually discussing here today. May we move on?"

"Yes, sir," Spaulding muttered, slouching in his seat.

Katrina snickered.

That was the moment he decided to stop talking in school. He told himself that keeping quiet and observing without interfering was a valuable skill in the researcher's arsenal. He was certainly becoming an expert at that.

Chapter Three

Note to Self: Also Avoid Cafeteria

At lunchtime, Spaulding wandered the cafeteria, wondering where to sit. He recognized most of the kids, but no one had been exactly friendly yet. He was reluctant to go up to someone and just strike up a conversation. Which was weird, because he'd never in his life hesitated to talk before.

He stopped to make a note of it: 12:10 p.m. *Observing changes in own behavior, possibly resulting from exposure to middle school environment.*

Nearby, Marietta sat at a table with Katrina and the rest of the sixth-grade popular girls. Spaulding slid into a seat at the table next to theirs. Marietta was bound to thaw out eventually, and then she could help him get to be friends with Katrina, too.

"Did you guys hear there was *another* big bonfire out by Blackhope Pond last night?" Katrina said loudly. "Oh, that's right, you wouldn't have, since, like, the police aren't telling anyone and my dad is practically the only person in town who knows about it and all." She flipped her hair over her shoulder while giving a no-big-deal kind of shrug.

Kenny Lin, a seventh-grader whom Spaulding had already pegged as another one of the populars, sat at the next table with a gang of the sporty kids. He tossed a soggy French fry onto Katrina's tray and gave her his usual wide, friendly grin. "Whatcha guys talking about?"

"Oh, hiii, Kenny!" Katrina said, batting her eyes rather ridiculously as if pretending she hadn't known he was there. "I was just telling everyone about a top-secret police investigation, that's all."

"*Whoa.*" Kenny scratched his head, mouth hanging open.

"I know, it's crazy!" Katrina said. "Daddy talked to a guy whose house is out in the woods who's asked the police to investigate but they aren't doing anything and he's totally going to sue if his house gets burned down and Daddy's gonna represent him."

"*Whoa,*" Kenny said again, mouth still agape. He stuffed in another fry and managed to chew while continuing to look dumbstruck.

Spaulding scowled at him behind his back. Apparently, around here a person didn't have to be insightful to be popular.

A skinny, pale, blonde girl named Grace Beely, who was sitting next to Katrina, chimed in next. Grace always drifted along in Katrina's wake and tended to say "Yeah" after everything Katrina said.

"Yeah," Grace said now, right on cue. Spaulding rolled his eyes. "And I heard it's all because of the old factory. My mom told me never to go near it—she says it's a haven for juvenile delinquents. She says Mr. Von Slecht needs to take responsibility and have it torn down."

Marietta sniffed and folded her arms. "That's ridiculous," she said. "Mr. Von Slecht is *very* responsible. If there was a problem with the factory, he'd take care of it. There aren't any juvenile delinquents sneaking in there."

Spaulding perked up. Here was a perfect opening for him to gather information while also impressing everyone with his firsthand observations. He cleared his throat. "I think something funny might be going on at the factory," he said. "I saw smoke coming out of the chimneys this morning." *Ha*—that ought to get their attention. He flipped open his notebook and pretended to be very busy with important note-taking.

Instantly, every head in the group swiveled toward his table and every pair of eyes fixed on him. Okay, maybe too much attention.

"Oh, *whoa*," Kenny said. "You know, they say that place is haunted." Solemnly, he held out a fry. "I'm Kenny."

Spaulding looked at the fry. It was squashed and greasy, and the fingers holding it appeared to be freshly licked. He took it anyway. "I'm S.S. Meriwether. My friends call me Boat."

Kenny wrinkled his nose. "*Boat?*" he asked around the

ketchup packet he was now sucking on. "What kind of a nick-name is that?"

"I'm glad you asked," Spaulding said, leaning in. "It's derived from the SS *Meriwether Lewis*, famed United States liberty ship in World War—"

Katrina yawned loudly. "Weren't you supposed to be tell-ing us about how you saw smoke coming from the factory?" she asked. "Not that you actually saw anything of the kind. It's abandoned, obviously."

"Yeah," Grace said. "Slecht-Tech is out of business, duh."

"Slecht-Tech is not out of business," Marietta snapped. She seemed to take this Slecht-Tech stuff personally. Spaulding made a note of it (after setting the limp fry aside and wiping his fingers thoroughly).

Katrina glared at her. "Oh my God, Mar, who cares? That's not the point."

"Well, my dad happens to work for them," Marietta said. "I just don't like people saying stuff about it that isn't true, that's all."

Spaulding kept scribbling notes. This was great—a source of inside information about the factory, right under his nose! Maybe he could get to the bottom of all the weird stuff going on, right here and now at lunch. That would really knock everybody's socks off. "I'm sure I saw smoke. Maybe you're wrong about the place being abandoned."

Marietta shook her head firmly, curls shaking. "No, it's

empty. They don't manufacture anything anymore—they have a fancy corporate office in town where they do computer stuff. That's where my dad works."

"Well, maybe somebody broke in."

"Juvenile delinquents," Grace said, eyes wide.

Marietta rolled her eyes. "There are electronic locks, a huge fence, and the windows are boarded up. No one broke in."

"I told you guys, it's *haunted,*" Kenny said. "I bet you it was, like, ghost smoke from the old days when the machines were still running."

"*Ghost smoke?*" Katrina eyed Kenny with a funny look on her face, but didn't say anything else. Spaulding had a feeling if anyone but Kenny had come up with the idea she'd have had plenty to say.

"Um . . . okay. Ghost smoke." Spaulding pretended to write it down. "I'll keep that in mind. Anyway, I saw something else weird, too. I heard you all talking about strange occurrences near Blackhope Pond before, so I went out there to investigate."

Katrina smiled and propped her chin on her hand. "Oh, this should be good. What'd you see?"

"There was this guy out there, right? Just *standing* there in the middle of the woods. Wearing a *suit.*"

"So, basically he was weird because he was dressed inappropriately for the setting." Katrina shot a significant look at Spaulding's own sweater vest and tie.

Spaulding felt a blush prickling over his face. "It wasn't only that. He chased me. Kind of. I think. And his hand—he grabbed my bike, and—and there were these bones . . ."

She sniffed and looked away, clearly unimpressed.

He hesitated. Should he tell her his theory? She'd think he was crazy. But as it stood now, she thought he'd been scared of some normal guy. If he told her what he suspected, maybe she'd be super impressed that he'd faced the living dead! How would he know if he didn't try?

"I think . . . I think he was dead," he said. "Well, undead." He grabbed the abandoned fry, shoved it in his mouth, and tried to chew in a relaxed-looking way.

There was an instant of stunned silence.

Then, as one, the whole group burst into hysterical laughter. The teacher on lunch duty shot them a dirty look. Only Kenny and Marietta were silent—Marietta because she was busy leaning as far away from Spaulding as she could without tumbling out of her seat; Kenny because his mouth was so far open it looked like his brain might be in danger of falling out.

"Oh my God," Katrina gasped. "You're serious!"

"I know it sounds strange," Spaulding said. "I just don't know how else to explain it. Actually, since you know the most about what's been happening in the woods, I thought maybe you— I mean, do you think the bonfires could be connected? Maybe someone's doing black magic? Or, um . . ."

Spaulding wasn't quite sure what the expression on

25

Katrina's face meant, but he was pretty sure it wasn't the look of someone about to give helpful information.

She cleared her throat, the corners of her mouth twitching. "You're saying you believe in magic?"

"More like witchcraft." The words were out before he could stop them. "I mean, I don't *believe* in it! I just research it." He shook his notebook at her, as proof of the seriousness of his work. But everyone was laughing too much to notice.

Katrina turned to Marietta. "You live near him, right? Do you know what's wrong with him?"

Marietta picked at her fingernails and shrugged.

Luckily, the bell rang at that moment, saving him from further humiliation. With a toss of her hair, Katrina picked up her lunch tray and made her way out of the cafeteria. The rest of her gang trotted obediently after her.

Kenny hesitated as if he was about to say something, but then his friends yelled for him to catch up, and he hurried away.

Only Marietta remained, fiddling with the garbage on her tray. Spaulding was still packing up his leftovers when he heard her whisper.

"*Psst.* Hey, you."

Spaulding glanced around. No one else was nearby. He raised his eyebrows at her.

She rolled her eyes. "*Duh, you,* obviously. Spaulding, or whatever."

"Boat," he corrected.

"I am not calling you Boat. And that's exactly the type of thing I want to talk to you about."

"Huh? My name?"

"That's not your name," she snapped, flattening her juice box so forcefully it squirted him. "You can't just decide you're going to be called that. Your name is your name."

He wiped some grape juice from his forehead. "Lots of people have nicknames."

"Yeah, cool people have nicknames that other people give them. That's not my point anyway." She rubbed a hand over her face and took a deep breath. "Just listen for a second, would you? I'm trying to tell you something."

He waited.

She stuffed the squashed juice box into the recycling bin, avoiding his eye. "I'm sorry if I've been mean to you. You seem nice and everything—that's why I decided to talk to you. I'm gonna tell you something, okay? But you can't tell anybody else."

He nodded. "I'm good at keeping secrets. And I don't have anyone to tell."

"Okay, so last year, in fifth grade? I was kind of a dork. Nobody liked me. Katrina picked on me. It sucked. Then, over the summer, we had swim team together and we got to be friends. And I figured out how to not act like such a doof. Now she's nice to me, and so's everybody else."

He frowned. "I'm happy for you and all, but why are you telling me?"

"I'm telling you to help you out." She slammed her tray onto the stack of other empty trays with a bang. "You can't just go around acting how you want, calling yourself what you want, talking crazy stuff about the rise of the living dead . . ."

"Oh." He scratched his head. "I can't?"

"No! You know how people always tell you 'just be yourself'? That's terrible advice. You won't survive middle school that way. Trust me. And now"—she held up a hand before he could reply—"we're done. That is the end of our one-time-only conversation."

Spaulding scowled. Maybe she was trying to help, but couldn't she be a little nicer about it? "It's not like I have a disease you're going to catch, Marietta."

"Oh, yes, you do." She gave him a half-pitying look over her shoulder as she headed for the doors. "Weird is totally transmissible by contact with the infected. Or that's what everyone else thinks, anyway, which amounts to the same thing."

With that, she was gone, and Spaulding was left alone in the cafeteria, staring at the doors swinging in her wake. He thought for a moment, then took out his notebook.

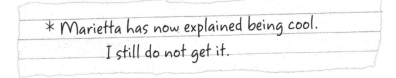

* Marietta has now explained being cool.
   I still do not get it.

Chapter Four

Note to Self: Watch Out For Giant Murderous Snakes

As usual, Spaulding walked home from the bus stop by himself. Marietta hurried up the street ahead of him the whole way, acting as though she didn't know he was there.

She turned off at an old Victorian two houses down from his. Like most houses in Thedgeroot, it was shabby on the outside. But a cheery glow shone from the windows, and smoke rose from the chimney. Someone was waiting for her. Probably her mom, with a batch of freshly baked cookies. That was what happened on TV commercials, anyway.

Spaulding kept walking, kicking irritably at sodden leaves plastered to the sidewalk.

At his house, the windows were dark, like they always were. Aunt Gwendolyn was no doubt in her study, plotting an untraceable jewel theft or an escape from a high-security mental ward or something. Personally, Spaulding thought her mystery novels were embarrassingly unrealistic, but somehow they were very popular.

Representative Sample of
Aunt Gwen's Books

(My offers to help come up with less unfortunate
titles have been rudely declined.)

Inside, he dumped his backpack on the floor and slammed the door so hard the stained-glass panel rattled. For a second he worried it would shatter, but then he shrugged. What difference would it make? It was already cracked.

He glared at the threadbare carpet as he kicked off his shoes. Stupid, rundown old house. Stupid, rundown, *creepy* old town.

"Spaulding?" Aunt Gwendolyn's voice floated to him from the far end of the dark-paneled hallway.

"Yes, Aunt Gwen?" he yelled.

"Nothing, just saying hello. You sounded like you were trying to bring the house down around our ears, so I thought perhaps you needed some acknowledgment."

"I'm fine." He wasn't ready to tell her that the school experiment had been a dismal failure. He knew she'd let him make his own decision, and she wouldn't criticize, but he didn't feel up to admitting it had been a mistake.

"Glad to hear it, dear. Heat up some of that leftover soup for your dinner, will you? Don't make one of your awful sandwiches."

Aunt Gwen had a well-established (and completely irrational) hatred for his favorite snack, potato-chip-and-jelly sandwiches. Although she left him to fend for himself in the kitchen most of the time, she expected him to make something with the healthy ingredients she brought home. He had to buy potato chips and white bread out of his own pocket money.

He pretended he hadn't heard and headed for the kitchen, where he did, in fact, fix himself a p.c.-and-j. Then he and his delicious creation went upstairs to his thinking spot on the roof of the side porch.

He laid out his sandwich, his schoolbooks, and a freshly sharpened pencil, and then cracked his knuckles. All set for some serious homework-doing. (Not that he had any real home-

The Thinking Spot

Pros:
- spacious
- private
- fresh air

Cons:
- splinters
- could fall to my death

work—he'd finished it on the bus. He was just setting himself work to keep his mind sharp.)

But he couldn't focus. Thoughts of school kept intruding—especially thoughts involving Katrina. He'd been so sure telling her about his paranormal research would impress her. What was he doing wrong? Why couldn't he seem to make friends?

Maybe Marietta was right and the problem was him—just him, being himself. How could he ever fix that?

He certainly couldn't ask Aunt Gwen for help; she was as hopeless socially as he was. He could call his parents . . . ha! *Right*. Advice on real-world situations was not exactly their specialty.

Sometimes having paranormal investigators for parents was the pits.

In fact, it was their fault he was having these problems at all. If they just did something normal for a living, they'd never have sent him to live with Aunt Gwen, and he'd have gone to public school his whole life, and he'd have all the friends he could possibly want.

As it was, their line of work wasn't good for anything but

embarrassing Spaulding. They weren't even that great at it. So they had a TV show. Big deal. It wasn't like they'd proven the existence of ghosts or demons or anything worthwhile.

With a sigh, he tossed his pencil down. He wasn't in the mood for homework anymore.

He slid farther down the roof and pulled up his collar, staring out at the weedy side yard and the abandoned house next door. It was an ugly view, but it suited his mood. That house was the neighborhood eyesore. Sunburned paint, piles of junk on the porch, gigantic snake on the roof, missing shingles—

Wait a second. He snapped bolt upright, throwing off his hood. Was he seeing things?

He scooted forward. A gnarled ash tree grew close beside the porch, and it was hard to get a look with its branches in the way. That was probably what he'd seen, come to think of it—just a really, thick, twisty branch that kind of looked like ...

A snake.

Make that a boa constrictor. It had to be ten feet long, probably more, and it looked as thick around as Spaulding's leg. It was coiled up, fast asleep in a patch of late-afternoon sunlight on the shingles.

Spaulding shook his head. *Unbelievable.* Boa constrictors on houses—just when he thought Thedgeroot couldn't get any more ridiculous.

He grabbed his notebook and flipped to a fresh page.

Does Thedgeroot have a boa
constrictor population?
Must research further.

He leaned over to check again. Still there, still dozing. Could it be dead?

At that moment, the snake twitched. Its tongue flicked out. It gave an enormous yawn, then curled into an even tighter spiral. Spaulding shivered. It was kind of cute, if you ignored the huge fangs and glistening, gaping throat.

Should he call the police? Animal control? That would be the responsible thing.

But if he did that, it would all be out of his hands. If something interesting were going on, he'd never know. Some stuffy official would show up and tell him to run along home like a good boy.

He needed a better look.

Cautiously, he crawled to the other side of the porch roof. Now he had a clear view, unobstructed by the ash tree. There was the ray of sunlight, there were the peeling shingles—and that was all. No snake.

But it couldn't have gone far; it hadn't had enough time. He'd just wait. Surely something so big would have to show itself again sooner or later. Tucking his hands into his pockets, he settled down against the wall of his house once more. Gradually, the evening fog rolled down over the trees, and a cold wind sprang up. He blew into his hands. There was no sign of the boa.

He had just decided to give up and go inside when a movement caught his eye. His gaze snapped back to the empty house.

But it wasn't the snake. Someone was inside. All he could make out through the window was a mop of black hair hanging over a sallow face. The figure glided by the window, staring straight ahead, and disappeared into the next room.

Spaulding's scalp tingled. Snakes, dead-or-possibly-not guys in the woods, and now a suspicious lurker in the abandoned house next door? Mysteries were practically falling into his lap!

He made up his mind. Forget Marietta's advice to blend in—that was never going to work for S.S. Meriwether. No, he was going to make a name for himself as an investigator or die trying. He'd be the kid who captured the giant snake, or proved the existence of the living dead, or *something*. If *that* didn't win him some friends, he didn't know what would.

* * *

This is the way we study our books,
study our books, study our books!
This is the way we study our books,
so earlyyyy in the moooorning!

But after that, it seemed Thedgeroot had made up its mind to be the most boring little town it could be. For days, Spaulding didn't encounter anyone any more out of the ordinary than Mrs. Welliphaunt—although she was certainly bad enough.

He didn't face any dangers

other than Katrina's sharp tongue—which, again, was quite bad enough.

And he saw nothing out of the ordinary in the house next door, even though he spent every afternoon in the thinking spot keeping watch.

He'd probably imagined the whole thing, he thought glumly one day as he sat watching the house yet again. The man in the suit, the snake, the figure in the house, all of it. Katrina was right, he was crazy and dumb and weird and—

"Hey!"

Spaulding flinched at the sudden yell and almost toppled

Peculiar child roaming streets yelling at people. Whatever happened to adult supervision??

"euphonium"?? Appears to be a tuba. Is she lying?

from his perch. He grabbed the edge of the roof to steady himself.

A girl had appeared at the side-yard fence. She looked about eight or nine, and she had a tuba case slung over her back that was nearly as tall as she was.

"Why are you up there spying on people?" she asked.

"I'm not spying, I'm thinking," he snapped.

"It looks exactly like spying. Can I help? Are you spying on ol' Mr. Radzinsky's house? Isn't that kinda boring, since it's empty?" She put down her tuba case and hooked her arms over the fence.

"I don't need help spying—I'm not spying, I mean. Who are you again?"

"I'm Lucy Bellwood. Marietta's sister. We live down the street. Hang on, let me just get Daphne over the fence, and I'll be right up."

"No! Why are you coming up? Why are you putting your tuba over the fence? And who's Daphne? Wait—is that what you call your tuba? That's a terrible name for a tuba."

She paused, the big black instrument case teetering atop the fence. "I'm coming up to help you! And where I go,

Daphne goes. She's not a tuba, she is a *euphonium*. Anyway, I hate stereotypes about tubas, even if she *was* a tuba. Which she isn't."

"Well, I don't need help. So don't come up." He folded his arms and tried to look stern. The last thing he needed was a little kid hanging around pestering him.

Lucy gazed up at him, her chin trembling.

He stayed stern for another second. Then his shoulders sagged. "All right," he sighed. "I suppose you can help by providing information."

She stuck her lip out. "Sounds boring."

"It's a very important job. Do you know anything about that empty house? Is someone buying it?"

Lucy gave up on heaving Daphne over the fence and hugged the case to her chest instead as she jigged up and down on her tip-toes. "Oh, I can give you all sorts of information about that! There's no way anybody's gonna buy that place, it's a dump. Nobody cleaned it up after ol' Mr. Radzinsky died."

"But there's someone in there right now."

She shook her head. "Nah. No one sets foot in there, 'cause everybody knows they never caught that snake of his after it ate him."

Spaulding's jaw dropped. "Are you kidding?"

"Nope! It was a few years ago. Nobody knows what happened to the snake afterward."

He was about to tell her he'd seen the reptile himself, but

at the last second held back. Maybe it was better not to tell anyone just yet.

Lucy glanced at her pink plastic watch and sighed. "Darn. I guess I better go before I'm late for my music lesson." She turned away. "But don't worry," she called over her shoulder, "I'll help with spying more later!"

Spaulding watched her run off up the street, the massive instrument case thumping on her legs. He shook his head. What a strange neighborhood. But at least now he knew where the mystery boa constrictor came from.

He also knew it was a killer.

*　*　*

Aunt Gwendolyn's study door was shut when he went inside. A closed door signaled that a character or even a whole plot was misbehaving, and she was not to be disturbed until she had the situation under control. It could be days.

For Spaulding, that meant one thing: potato-chips-and-jelly sandwich free-for-all. Maybe even double-deckers. He deserved it.

After he made dinner (not only a double, but also strawberry jelly with jalapeño chips—a new and excitingly risky combination), he went straight to his room.

He didn't allow himself even a glance at his thinking spot as he passed. He wasn't in the mood to think about shadowy figures or killer serpents or creepy guys in suits. He was accumulating quite a collection of things *not* to think about, actually.

However, trying not to think about things isn't a good recipe for a restful night's sleep. (Also not a good recipe, as it turned out: strawberry-jelly-and-jalapeño-chip sandwiches.)

Chef Meriwether's Classic
Strawberry Jelly-and-Jalapeño Chip Sandwich

· 2 slices white bread
· Lots of Strawberry jelly
· Very generous handful
  jalapeño chips

Note to Self: **NO** DO NOT MAKE AGAIN

After lying in the dark for some time, thinking every creak was the sound of the snake coming to eat him, Spaulding couldn't stand it anymore. He sat up and threw off the blankets. Maybe a sip of water would help.

He shuffled into the hallway. Outside, the dark shape of the house next door loomed. It seemed closer than it did in daylight, somehow. Almost like it was peering in through the window at him, instead of the other way around.

He forced himself to look away. He was being ridiculous.

But . . . there *was* something odd about it, wasn't there? Something out of place.

The window—that was it. The window was lit by a faint greenish glow. The shadows in the room shifted and jumped like someone was walking around in there with a candle.

He *had* to find out what was going on. A little voice in the back of his mind suggested it might just possibly be a bad idea to sneak into a house where some unknown person was creeping around after midnight, but he tamped it down.

He went back to his room and yanked on his sneakers, then hurried downstairs, tiptoeing carefully past Aunt Gwendolyn's study.

But Aunt Gwen had finally emerged.

As he passed the living room doorway, she looked up from her book—something with spaceships and laser-gun-wielding aliens on the cover—and frowned at his sneaker-clad feet. "Going out at this time of night, Spaulding? Whatever for?"

"Research," he said shortly. "Has to be under cover of darkness."

"*Research?*" She stared at him. Then she turned back to her book. "In that case, best get my flashlight from the hall table—fresh batteries."

Spaulding grinned. You had to say that for Aunt Gwen: she understood research.

"Oh, and Spaulding," she called after him.

He glanced back.

Aunt Gwen gave him a look over her glasses. "Be back in a half-hour on the dot. I'm willing to assume you're not up to anything silly, but I don't want you wandering all over town. And if you're late, I'm afraid I'll have to make you face . . . *the fan mail.*" She gave an evil-villain chuckle.

Spaulding squinted at her. "You wouldn't by any chance be looking for an excuse to put me on fan mail duty, would you?" He and Aunt Gwen both loathed fan mail duty—Aunt Gwen's fans tended to be weird, and if they didn't get detailed replies, they wrote back. *Often.*

Aunt Gwen batted her eyes innocently behind her crooked glasses. "Of course not! I just have to make the consequences severe or you won't take me seriously."

Spaulding covered up a smile. It *was* kind of hard to take Aunt Gwen seriously. Currently she was wearing an old fedora, her bathrobe, and cowboy boots. "Fine. But I'm noting the time. You're not going to pull a fast one and claim I was late so you can stick me with extra letters. *Again.*"

Aunt Gwen gasped. "I would *never!*"

After a brief delay while the contract was drawn up, Spaulding raced up the street toward the house next door. Inside, the light was still visible. As he watched, it drifted across the front windows and disappeared on the far side of the house. He'd have to move fast while he knew whoever-it-was was out of the way.

Spaulding Meriwether will
not have to answer fan mail
unless he returns home later
than 12:36 a.m. Gwendolyn
Meriwether hereby swears not
to tamper with the clocks.

Signed,
G. Meriwether

He tested the knob on the side door—stiff, but it opened. He held his breath for a moment, afraid someone would have heard the creak. All was silent. He slipped inside.

He was in a tiny mudroom, bare except for a few boxes and a coat rack. To the left, a door opened into a dark and empty living room. The intruder must have either gone upstairs or down the hall, but there was no way to tell which. The house was still perfectly quiet—oddly quiet. Shouldn't he hear a footstep, or squeaking floorboard, or something?

Just then, the shadows on the staircase shifted. A green glow washed over the walls and ceiling. Someone was coming downstairs.

Spaulding needed a hiding place—fast.

He backed up a step, but there was something behind his foot. Something he was sure hadn't been there before. It felt cylindrical and heavy, like a log, but immovable.

There wasn't time to get his balance. In an instant he was flat on his back, the air knocked from his lungs, his head ringing. As he lay stunned, the log-like thing slid out from under his calves.

And then it popped up right in front of his nose. He caught a whiff of something much like Aunt Gwen's ancient alligator purse (he always *had* hated that thing).

It was the snake. The snake with a history of eating people—people who fed it and were its friends even, whereas Spaulding was *not* its friend, not even an acquaintance, really—

The snake opened its jaws wide. The smell washed over Spaulding again. His stomach churned. Boy, if he ever made it home again, that stupid purse was going straight into the garbage.

"There, there, my dearest," crooned a hollow voice from somewhere nearby. "Don't be frightened."

Chapter Five

Note to Self: Add House Next Door to List of Places to Avoid

Spaulding sat up and scuttled across the floor, looking around for the speaker and keeping an eye on the snake at the same time. "Who's that?" he called. "Where are you?"

"Stupid as well as nosy," the voice said. "I should have you arrested for breaking and entering. Get out, before I give David the command to attack."

The greenish light had appeared at the door to the mudroom. Someone must be standing there with a flashlight or glowstick or something. He held up a hand to shield his eyes, squinting.

And then he understood.

It wasn't a person shining a light in his eyes. It was a person *giving off* light. In fact, it was the person he had seen in the house before—the weirdo with the crazy hair. Only now he seemed to be fluorescent.

"You glow in the dark," Spaulding said unnecessarily.

The figure gave a snort. "Brilliant deduction, Mr. Holmes. Astound and delight us with another, won't you? I said *get out!*"

"But I thought no one lived here." Spaulding's head ached, and it took him a moment to understand the obvious. "Wait, are you . . . Mr. Radzinsky?"

"Who wants to know? Are you selling something? Come here, dearest." The snake gave one last threatening hiss before returning to its master, speeding across the floor with a sound like leaves blowing across pavement.

Spaulding wiped his palms on his jeans. He wished he dared take out his notebook and jot down every detail. This guy was clearly dead, but also quite different from the man in the suit. That meant Spaulding had now discovered two distinct varieties of undead. His parents hadn't managed that in ten years of their idiotic TV show.

What he needed to do now was stay on the ghost's good side. Then he could come back with a camera and get some solid proof. He had a feeling he'd better be as polite as possible—Mr. Radzinsky seemed a bit testy.

"Thanks for not calling the police, sir. I only came in because I saw someone inside. I thought it might be vandals."

"Oh." The ghost scratched at his chin, which made Spaulding notice the rather gray and peeling quality of his complexion. Where his eyes should have been, there were nothing but two deep wells of shadow, each with a tiny spark of green light deep within.

"You needn't have bothered; I'm well protected by my dear David Boa." Mr. Radzinsky gave the snake a pat, his hand passing right through its scales.

Mr. Radzinsky
Somehow appears to be slightly on the decomposing side, despite not having an actual body.

Spaulding nodded and smiled weakly at the snake. Mr. Radzinsky seemed to be relaxing a little. Spaulding tried to think of some small talk appropriate for chatting with a spirit.

"So, how is it you're still liv—I mean, still here? Everyone in the neighborhood seems to think you, y'know . . . went away."

The hand that had been petting the boa constrictor stilled. The ghost stared at Spaulding from the blank pools of his eyes. Something started to happen to his face. The skin shriveled away from his eye sockets. His lips cracked and peeled back. Spaulding found himself facing a yellowed, grinning skull.

"I'm not a fool, you know," the skull said through its teeth. "I *do* realize I'm dead."

"Of course, sir. I was only trying to broach the subject politely."

Before Spaulding could even blink, the ghost was right in his face.

"You can't bring up my death *politely*." His voice dropped to a hiss. David reared up beside him, also hissing. "I see now—you're here to laugh at me, aren't you?"

A faint rattling began to build, coming from all sides. Spaulding darted a glance around. The windows and doors trembled. Some unseen force was shaking the whole house.

"No! I'd just like to talk to you. For research."

Mr. Radzinsky's face—his eyeballs shriveled into little gray raisins, his mouth stretched hideously wide, as if he'd unhinged his jaw—remained frozen, inches away.

The boa constrictor began to twine around Spaulding's body, starting at the ankles and working its way up. He tried to dislodge it, but it was too strong.

And then Mr. Radzinsky spoke. "Research, you say?" He leaned back, looking thoughtful. "I myself did a great deal of research. The brilliance of my work was never recognized, but I did have a number of irate letters-to-the-editor published in various periodicals. I suppose as a fellow researcher, it wouldn't be right to kill you, even if you were trespassing."

The snake's death grip loosened slightly. Spaulding had just enough air to squeak, "Much appreciated, sir—if you could just call off your snake—"

The ghost chuckled. "Oh, goodness, don't be frightened of David. He wouldn't harm a flea."

"But he *ate* you," Spaulding blurted out.

Mr. Radzinsky flapped a hand at him. "Shh! He bears a lot of guilt about that! He wouldn't have done it if he hadn't been suffering from an undiagnosed mood disorder. I blame myself. Anyway, it was for the best. I have the peace and quiet I never had in life, and we're closer than ever."

This was about the creepiest thing Spaulding had ever heard. He was fond of animals himself, but it seemed like you should draw the line once they ate you alive.

David Boa finally uncoiled himself, but he didn't go far. He just slid down Spaulding's torso and draped himself across Spaulding's lap, soaking up his warmth. Spaulding tried to look like he wasn't bothered by the snake's cold weight pinning him down.

The ghost tilted his head, his face slowly returning to normal as he gazed at Spaulding and the snake. "You know, I've just had a thought," Mr. Radzinsky said. "Since I'm choosing to let you live, you are indebted to me."

Spaulding gulped. Based on his readings, you didn't want restless spirits expecting favors from you. If you failed to help them, you could be in for a severe haunting. But telling Mr. Radzinsky no also seemed dangerous.

"I don't know many—well, *any*—living people these days," Mr. Radzinsky continued, "and I have certain . . . *uses* . . . for someone in possession of flesh and blood."

Uses? Flesh and blood? This was not sounding good.

"Gee, sir," Spaulding said, trying to subtly shift David Boa off his lap, "I'd like to help, of course, but right now my aunt is expecting me back any minute."

Mr. Radzinsky's eyes narrowed to slits.

"It's just, if I don't get back on time I'll be grounded, and then it'll be hard for me to get out of the house again, which would mean I couldn't help you for a long time."

The ghost folded his arms. He still didn't look entirely pleased, but at least the house wasn't shaking. Spaulding figured that was about the best that could be expected. "Very well," Mr. Radzinsky said. "But you do agree to our arrangement?"

Spaulding slipped out from under David and backed toward the door quickly. "Well, I'll try, but—"

Instantly, Mr. Radzinsky reared back and somehow *expanded* until he was towering over Spaulding. His green glow turned a threatening shade of orange.

Spaulding panicked. Before he knew it, he found himself gabbling, "I agree! I agree! It's a deal!"

The ghost soundlessly clapped his hands together. "Brilliant! Do hurry back, then, and we'll settle the details."

Spaulding dove through the door and into the blessedly ghost-free outdoors.

Behind him, Mr. Radzinsky's voice echoed faintly, "And I will hold you to your word."

The door slammed of its own accord, and Spaulding stared back at the silent house. Goose bumps prickled up his arms. What exactly had he just agreed to?

* * *

He'd hoped he'd wake up in the morning feeling better. But even by the light of day, he couldn't stop thinking about Mr. Radzinsky and the deal they'd made. What could a ghost need help with? Hopefully not wreaking a terrible vengeance on the living or anything like that. In folklore, revenge always seemed to be a pretty big concern for the dead.

Not really the kind of thing I want to get involved with.

"This is ridiculous," Spaulding muttered around the fingernail he was chewing as he sat up in bed. "I just won't go back there. Problem solved! That is, as long as he's trapped in his house and can't come here and get me."

He thought of Mr. Radzinsky's mood flipping to rage in an instant, his face hollowing into a rotted husk, the walls of the

Mr. Radzinsky & David Boa in a good mood.

Mr. Radzinksy & David Boa miffed.

house quaking . . . He shivered. There was no knowing what such a creature might be capable of. Problem possibly not solved.

A sudden stinging in his thumb made him realize he'd chewed the nail down to the quick without noticing. He sighed.

It was time to admit it: he needed help. And there were only two people in the world he could think of who might just possibly believe him.

He picked up his cell phone, took a deep breath, and dialed.

It only rang once before a breathy, fake-accented voice swept over him. "Serena Meriwether speaking. Pray tell me, caller, do you hail from this world, or the astral plane?"

He held back a sigh. The accent meant she was in TV-star-Serena mode, even if there wasn't a camera around. "Hi, Mom. Doesn't your phone show who's calling?"

"Oh, hello, darling! Of course I felt it would be you calling—but one never knows, does one?" Serena said. She sounded distracted. But then, she almost always sounded that way. She tended to multitask.

"Um, no, I guess one doesn't," Spaulding said, trying to be agreeable instead of arguing about the likelihood of getting a phone call from the astral

Serena Multitasking

(Serena's version of multitasking involves many assistants.)

plane. "Anyway, could you help me with something, Mom? Something happened last night—"

"Mm-hmm . . . no, no, I said no sugar and extra ice—take that one away, please . . . and how's school, sweetie? Do you like Thedgeroot? It sounds so quaint."

"That's part of what I wanted to talk to you about. It's kind of a weird town, Mom. I think you guys should come check it out."

Serena laughed. "Oh, sweetie."

"I'm serious! I really think if you were going to find true paranormal activity anywhere, you'd find it here. There're some really weird people around, and I think someone might be doing black magic, and—"

"Darling, I know how much you've always wanted to be on the show. But it just wouldn't work out."

"I'm not trying to get on the show. I don't want to be on the show! I just hoped you could come help me investigate—"

"I've even mentioned it to the producers," Serena continued over him, "but they say a child character just wouldn't be a good fit for the show. I'm so sorry, Spuddy."

Spaulding gritted his teeth. "A child character? You mean, your actual child?"

"You know perfectly well what I mean." She sighed, a hint of frustration creeping into her voice. "Anyway, this isn't coming from me, it's those awful producers. They think your character—sorry, you—would be a bit too, well . . . boring. We'd lose viewers."

"They said that?"

"Actually, they said boring and weird. But not in a bad way! It's just not good for TV."

"Boring and—that's ridiculous!" he sputtered. "They've only ever met me once. What do they know?"

"You have to admit, when you came to visit you didn't make the best impression. All you brought with you were textbooks and a teddy bear. Not even a change of clothes. It did make you seem a trifle odd."

"I was only eight! Aunt Gwen should've helped me pack. And those were books on the paranormal so I could help you with research."

"That's beside the point anyway, darling." Serena dropped her voice to a mysterious whisper. "You know why we can't have you live with us—the dark entities we confront are far too dangerous to expose you to."

"You haven't confronted a dark entity once," Spaulding burst out. He knew he wasn't going to get anywhere by getting upset, but she was so infuriating. "It's all camera tricks. The show's ridiculous, if you want to know the truth—I'd never be on it even if you begged me!"

"Spaulding, really! I know you're angry, but you know better than to make light of what we do. Skepticism invites demons in. Touch wood and turn clockwise three times right this instant."

"Ugh!" He held the phone away from his ear and glared at it. "I'm turning counterclockwise, Mother, even as we speak."

Serena sighed loudly. "You're being very childish, Spaulding."

He scowled. For once, she was saying something true. With an effort, he pulled himself together. "Look, I called about something important, if you'd just listen. Do you know what I did last night? I *talked to a ghost!* How's that for boring, huh?"

There was a long silence. Finally, Serena spoke very quietly. "Spudling, sweetheart. We've been over this before. You mustn't try to get attention this way. Remember when you thought you'd recorded a banshee wailing?"

Heat swept over his face. Of course she had to bring that up. "That was different—I was just a little kid. This time—"

"It turned out to be Aunt Gwen's snoring echoing through an air vent in your room. Our team spent a lot of time analyzing that recording, and it was all a waste. Not a scrap of material we could use on the show. And thank goodness we realized before it aired! We'd have been laughingstocks."

"But this time—"

She cut him off. "I'm so sorry, darling, but I just don't have time to chat anymore right now. We're ready to start taping. I'll call tonight, all right? No more fibs. Good-bye, sweetie, kiss ki—"

Spaulding ended the call. His face was burning—he wasn't sure if it was more from anger or embarrassment. He should never have called. He'd known they'd never consider coming to Thedgeroot to help him.

But even expecting a no, he hadn't expected to be humiliated.

Spaulding gave serious consideration to never getting out of bed again, but eventually his stomach started to growl. Maybe he'd feel better after a nice, relaxing breakfast over the morning paper.

Downstairs, he made cinnamon toast, sat down at the kitchen table, and started leafing through the newspaper. But then a small article buried in the second section caught his eye, and breakfast suddenly got a lot less relaxing.

Police Helpless as Rash of Grave Robberies Continues

THEDGEROOT-- More disturbed graves were found this week in Thedgeroot Cemetery, reports an anonymous source. While groundskeepers work overtime to fill in graves and clean up piles of earth before cemetery visitors see them, police have been trying to keep the gruesome incidents out of the public—

not the first time graves have been tampered with in recent months, the source reports, and the epidemic is not limited to Thedgeroot. Similar incidents have been reported throughout the tri-county area. Police seem no closer to solving the case, or to determining a possible motive. Thedgeroot PD could not be —hed for comment.

"Ew," he mumbled through a mouthful of toast. Then it hit him. Disturbed graves. The man in the suit.

What if Spaulding hadn't been crazy to think he was dead? What if graves were being disturbed . . . by the dead themselves?

If he was right, then the police were way off base with their investigation. They should be looking for someone doing black magic to raise the dead, not some ring of regular crooks robbing graves—

He laid the paper down and stared into space as another realization sank in: he had the pieces he needed to solve all his problems. He just had to put them together right.

Sure, he was stuck in a town where something paranormal and possibly dangerous was going on. And yes, everyone he knew thought he was either crazy or weird, including his own parents. But the truth was he, and he alone, had met a real ghost and knew that the living dead stalked the streets of Thedgeroot.

All he had to do was prove it.

After that, everyone would realize he wasn't weird at all. Katrina would think he was cool and interesting; Marietta wouldn't be embarrassed to talk to him in public. His parents would be forced to admit he was a better paranormal investigator than they'd ever be. They'd be begging him to live with them.

The first step would be to track down the man in the suit. If he was just some homeless guy, he was probably camped out somewhere by the pond, and Spaulding would know his theory was wrong.

But if he was a reanimated corpse . . . well, Spaulding would be ready to snap a picture and score his first piece of solid proof.

* * *

The trail where Spaulding had last seen the man in the suit wasn't hard to find again. The woods around it were tangled and dark, and the dirt path stood out clearly; everywhere else the undergrowth was too thick to pass through.

In a muddy spot a few feet down the trail, prints from a narrow, smooth-soled shoe were visible. Spaulding was no expert on tracking, but they seemed like the kind of shoe an old guy would wear with a nice suit. It seemed that if he wanted to track down the man in the suit, he was going to have to follow that path into the woods.

Spaulding hesitated. Why was it that everything around Thedgeroot seemed to happen in the woods? Couldn't just one single mysterious event happen in a nice, well-lit, populated area in the middle of town?

"Hey!"

Spaulding spun around to see Lucy Bellwood speeding toward him on her bike like an oncoming train. Coming up behind him and shouting "Hey!" seemed to be turning into a regular hobby for her.

He smoothed his hair and tried to arrange his face into a

calm, cool expression, like someone who had definitely not just been startled out of his skin.

"Fancy meeting you here," Lucy panted as she screeched to a halt inches short of smashing into him.

"By which she means, we saw you riding out here and she insisted on following you," said Marietta, pulling up behind her sister.

Lucy's cheeks reddened. "Shut up, Marietta."

"You shut up, Ludwig!"

Spaulding raised an eyebrow. "Ludwig?"

Lucy heaved a long-suffering sigh. "Oh, she finds it incredibly funny to call me Ludwig, because I play the piano—Ludwig van Beethoven, you know?"

He nodded, impressed. "Good nickname. Anyway, I'm glad you're here." He smiled at her. She turned even redder. "I was just doing some research. Maybe you two could help."

"Research?" Marietta narrowed her eyes. "Is this about that guy you thought was a zombie?"

"A zombie?" Lucy gasped. "Here? What? Where?" She swiveled her head frantically, as if she wasn't sure whether to run for her life or get an autograph.

"Don't be ridiculous," Spaulding said quickly. "I never said anything about zombies." He folded his arms and tried to look dignified. If only he hadn't picked today to wear his *Ghostbusters* T-shirt—Marietta would probably start telling everyone he thought the movie was a documentary. "He was a revenant, if anything."

Lucy's face fell. "Like a church guy?"

"Not a *reverend*, doofus—*revenant*," Marietta said. "But it means the same thing. You just don't want to admit you're talking about zombies," she said to Spaulding.

Spaulding scowled. "There's a difference. I don't mean there's some kind of rage virus or something making dead people wander around eating brains. That's crazy. I just think someone might be using black magic to raise the dead."

She rolled her eyes. "Huge difference. Got it. So you're out here looking for zom—sorry, *revenants*?"

Spaulding decided now would be a good time to practice not telling everyone everything all the time. "I'm simply following this trail to see where it goes."

Lucy bounced on her bicycle seat eagerly. "I can help! I know my way all around here." She raced past him to lead the way down the path. "Marietta and I used to explore the woods all the time, back when we were investigating the secrets of Thedgeroot."

Marietta looked mortified. "Shut up, Ludwig!" she snapped, pedaling after her quickly.

The narrow path sloped gradually upward into the hills. Eventually, it connected with a dirt road, just wide enough for a single vehicle. Fresh tire tracks crisscrossed in the mud. The smooth-soled shoeprints showed up again too, but so did lots of other footprints. Any of them could be from the man in the suit, or none of them. It seemed to be an awfully well-used road for a dirt track in the middle of nowhere.

Lucy stopped at the edge of the road. "Which way do you wanna go? That way's a shortcut back to town."

"Hmm." He looked down the road the way she pointed, then peered at the ground. In the muddle of footprints, a single smooth-soled shoeprint showed clearly, heading the opposite direction. "What if you go the other way?"

Lucy shrugged. "Not much. If you go for a really long ways you get to the old mine, but there's nothing there now except some filled-in tunnels. There's no way in—we've looked. The only other thing out there is the factory."

Spaulding straightened up fast. "The factory?"

"Yeah. The road doesn't go too close, but you can see it."

The man in the suit had been headed toward the factory? Now *that* was worth investigating. Spaulding jumped back onto his bike. "Let's go."

Marietta mumbled something under her breath about a colossal waste of time, but Lucy and Spaulding ignored her.

As the dirt road took them deeper into the woods, it quickly became steep and narrow. Spaulding began to pant. Stupid man in the suit. Couldn't he just stay in town where everything was all paved and civilized?

"How . . . much . . . farther?" he gasped at Lucy.

She skidded to a halt. "No farther," she said, not even a little winded. "Look!"

He raised his head. Up ahead, the trees thinned abruptly.

While he'd been focused on trying not to have a heart attack, they had come out of the hills to the edge of a valley.

A few hundred yards away stood the factory behind its high fence. The smokestacks weren't smoking now, if they ever had been. The way the lowering clouds were billowing over the tops of the stacks made him wonder if it might have just been fog the other time, too.

"Wow, look at that." Marietta ambled over and folded her arms. "Why, it's big and cement and gray. I am *sooo* glad we came out here to look closer."

Spaulding scowled. It didn't seem too promising, he had to admit.

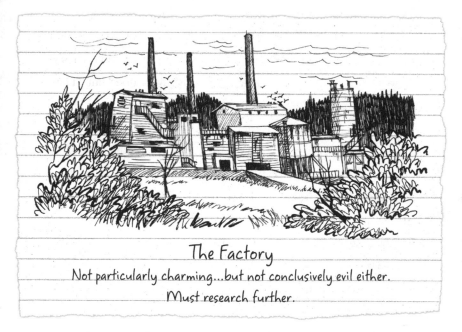

The Factory
Not particularly charming...but not conclusively evil either.
Must research further.

He hadn't expected a big sign saying EVIL DELIVERY ENTRANCE HERE or anything, but some sort of discovery would have been nice. Especially with other people standing there expectantly, looking all smirky and superior (Marietta) or crushingly disappointed (Lucy).

He gave the fence a half-hearted rattle. The chain link was probably climbable, but the curls of razor wire along the top didn't look very inviting. Marietta followed him through the long grass and leaned on the fence a few feet away.

"You've never been in there with your dad or anything?" he asked.

"Nope. It's been closed as long as I can remember."

"What did they make out here in the old days?"

"Well, first it was a refinery, back when the Von Slechts owned a big gold mine. Then the mines shut down—they'd gone so deep it was too expensive to get the gold out. They switched over to manufacturing stuff until old Mr. Von Slecht died and his son decided to close the factory."

Spaulding kicked the fence, only half-listening. What a bust. He'd been sure if he got near the place there'd be some clue or—

A scream ripped through the silence.

Spaulding and Marietta spun around, scanning the woods and fields. Nothing moved.

"Wait," Marietta gasped. "Where's Lucy?"

Spaulding was sure she'd been right behind them when

they'd walked up to the fence, but there was no sign of her now. Her bike lay in the road with theirs, abandoned.

"Maybe she went farther into the woods," he said. They stared across the road at the shadowy trees.

"You go first," Marietta said.

"She's your sister," Spaulding said.

Luckily, before the ethical debate got heated, they heard the *slap-slap* of running feet. Lucy appeared around a bend in the road. She tripped over the bikes and went sprawling in the dirt as Spaulding and Marietta raced up to her.

"Are you okay, Lud?" Marietta knelt beside her and patted Lucy's back. "Are you hurt?"

Lucy looked up, eyes huge and hair full of twigs and leaves. "There's a dead guy back there!"

Marietta switched gears instantly from concern to annoyance. "*That's* what all the screeching was about? Some stupid thing you imagined? You had me really worried!" She hauled Lucy to her feet and dusted her off with a few violent swats. Then she wheeled on Spaulding. "See what you've done? You've warped her little brain with all your dead people talk."

Spaulding grabbed Lucy's shoulder. "I believe you, Lucy. Quick, show me where you saw it."

Lucy nodded eagerly and trotted off the way she'd come. Spaulding followed, dragging Marietta along by the sleeve.

They rounded the bend in the road. Lucy pointed toward a shallow ditch across the way, where brambles and weeds grew in a dense tangle. There was something else there too, something dark and lumpy. It blended in so well, it was no wonder they'd ridden past it without noticing before.

"See? See?" Lucy demanded. "You can admit I was right anytime now."

Marietta gasped, then clamped a hand over her nose. "Id is a body!"

Spaulding leaned in for a closer view. Dark suit, gloves— make that glove, singular. The

Maybe just resting?
(although the flies seem like a bad sign)

other was shredded to bits, and most of the fingers that should have been in it were gone, too. "This is him! This is the guy I was looking for!"

Marietta wrinkled her forehead, still holding her nose. "You doh dis guy?"

"This is the guy I saw out by the pond before. When I read about the grave robberies, I figured—"

"Whoa, whoa, whoa. Since wed are there grabe robbers idbolved? You didn't thig you should bention thad little detail to us?"

"It was in the newspaper! It's really everyone's own responsibility to keep up with current events. And stop holding your nose, he doesn't smell."

Lucy looked cheerful again. "This is so exciting! What do we do now?"

Marietta folded her arms. "We do nothing now. There's a psycho on the loose digging up graves, and we're not getting mixed up in it."

"Come oonnn," Lucy whined.

"We're just doing a little research," Spaulding said. "Maybe a stakeout. We won't do anything dangerous."

"We won't, huh?" Marietta stabbed a finger at his nose, then at the corpse. "Haven't you noticed we already are in danger? Whoever killed this guy might still be around."

Lucy gave a whimper, but Spaulding held up a hand. "Calm down, Marietta—he wasn't murdered."

She glared at him. "Oh, no?"

"No, because he's not really dead. Or, I mean, he is, but walking-around-dead, not regular dead." He picked up a stick and gave the corpse an experimental nudge. "Wake up!"

The stick sunk into the man's side with an unpleasant squelch. He showed no signs of moving.

Marietta slapped his hand. "Stop poking that thing! Let's go. You can tell us all about your hallucinations after we get home and call the police."

"I'm telling you, he's going to move. Hang on . . . I need to get my camera. I have to get proof . . ."

He ran back down the road to the bikes, the girls close behind.

"Fine," Marietta said as he rooted through his bag. "You can get your picture on our way past, but we're not—"

The sound of voices nearby interrupted her.

"Well, I am very sorry you feel I'm doing such a bad job," a woman's voice said sharply. "I'd like to see you try supervising—"

"Silence!" A second, deeper voice cut off the first, and a man and woman stepped out of the trees a few feet away. The man jerked his head in their direction.

Kind of like seeing a giraffe
& a bulldog out for a walk together
(if the giraffe & the bulldog weren't dressed
appropriately for the outdoors at all).

"What are you children doing here?" the bulldog man demanded. He didn't sound angry, exactly—more like he was used to getting answers to his questions, and quickly. The woman was silent, her narrow, ice-blue eyes unblinking.

Spaulding cleared his throat. "We're riding our bikes? Sir? And this isn't private land, so, I mean—is this private land? Uh . . ." Darn it. He wasn't coming across nearly as confident as he'd intended. Talking to people who looked so important and rich made him feel small and unworthy.

A sharp finger poked his ribs. "Be polite," Marietta hissed. "Don't you know who that is?"

He gave her a blank look. Since he obviously didn't know who it was, she took over the talking duties.

"We're sorry, Mr. Von Slecht, Dr. Darke, we didn't mean to trespass—and we weren't doing anything or anything—and we were just leaving and everything . . ."

Spaulding didn't know if he was more surprised by meeting the mysterious owner of Slecht-Tech out in the woods or by seeing Marietta reduced to a blithering idiot by his mere presence.

Mr. Von Slecht sniffed and gave a grand sort of nod, as if granting them permission to continue existing. "See that it doesn't happen again. Run along now."

"Yessir!" Marietta grabbed her bike and raised her eyebrows at Spaulding and Lucy to do the same. "Thank you, sir!"

Von Slecht made a little shooing motion with his fingers.

"One does like to see children that respect authority, eh, Darke?" he said, turning back to the doctor.

Spaulding glanced back out of the corner of his eye, taking his time to follow Lucy and Marietta. Von Slecht seemed to have forgotten their existence the instant he dismissed them, but the doctor was still watching them.

"As I was saying," Von Slecht began, "if you're going to keep losing track—"

"Shh!" Dr. Darke hissed, elbowing him sharply. "Not now!"

Von Slecht rubbed his side and grumbled. The doctor ignored him. She glared at Spaulding, who suddenly felt like he should be pedaling a lot faster. Marietta and Lucy were already out of sight around the next corner. As he caught up to them, Lucy gasped and slammed on her brakes. Marietta and Spaulding swerved to avoid crashing into her.

"What—where—it—" Lucy gabbled. She pointed into the bushes where they'd found the man in the suit.

Only now, the body was gone.

Chapter Seven

Note to Self:
STOP BOTHERING GHOSTS!!!

The thinking spot turned out to have room for three, although the extra occupants did make the roof creak alarmingly, and nobody had much shoulder room. As soon as Spaulding shut the window behind them so there was no danger Aunt Gwen would overhear, everyone began talking at once.

"One at a time," he yelled over Marietta and Lucy. "First off, we need to organize our thoughts." He flipped his notebook open to a fresh page.

1. Why was the man in the suit near the factory?

2. Why were Mr. Von Slecht and that lady out in the woods?

3. How are revenants and Slecht-Tech connected?

4. Who is that lady, anyway?

"That's Dr. Darke," Marietta said, reading over his shoulder. "Mr. Von Slecht's business partner. And there's nothing suspicious about them being out for a walk. We were the ones trespassing."

"We were not," Lucy argued. "Nobody owns those woods. Spaulding's right—they were acting weird. Why did they want us to leave?"

"They probably thought we were going to vandalize something. You know, you just so happen to be talking about our father's employer. Mr. Von Slecht is a very intelligent, hard-working, successful—"

"See, she's not gonna be able to think straight about this," Lucy interrupted. "She's got a huge crush on him."

"I do not!"

"Yeah huh. He's her hero 'cause he's a big business-guy and she wants to start a business someday."

Marietta pressed her lips into a tight line and scowled into the distance.

Spaulding giggled, then tried to cover it with a cough. "Okay then, how do you explain

Dora M. Mitchell

that the dead guy was in the woods right by their factory at the same time they were out there?"

Marietta sniffed. "Circumstantial evidence. A judge would laugh you out of court with this stuff."

"Legal junk," Lucy broke in again. "That's her other thing, besides economics and local history. She likes really boring stuff."

"Can we please focus on the important thing?" Marietta snapped. "We just found a *dead body*. And Crazy Pants over here wants to say it's no big deal because he was a revenant."

"I didn't say it wasn't a big deal—I just said there weren't murderers lurking in the woods. The guy had already *been* dead. We weren't in any danger."

"The problem is, no one but you believes in the living dead. You do realize that, right?" She shook the notebook at him. "And yet here you've already concluded that there *are* revenants, and that they're connected to Slecht-Tech. Real investigators don't jump to conclusions."

"I believe him!" Lucy protested. Spaulding and Marietta ignored her.

"I admit I haven't found hard evidence yet." He grabbed the notebook back and updated the list.

2. Why were Mr. Von Slecht and that lady out in the woods?
ARE there revenants, and if so
3. ~~How~~ are revenants and Slecht-Tech connected?

4. Who is that lady, anyway?

"See? No jumping! So now let's find out if I'm right once and for all by staking out the cemetery."

"No way." Marietta jumped to her feet. "I already told you, we're done. Out. Good-bye." She started to stomp off to finalize her grand exit. Then she hesitated. "Um . . . how do you get down from here, exactly?"

"Wait!" Spaulding burst out.

She glanced at him expectantly. "Yeah? What?"

He thought fast, eyes darting around for inspiration. There had to be some way he could convince her to believe him. If she left now, still thinking he was crazy, he had a feeling she'd avoid him forever. His gaze landed on the house next door.

"What if . . ." he leaned forward and lowered his voice, "I could show you absolute proof that the paranormal exists?"

She narrowed her eyes. "Like what?"

"If I just tell you, you'll say I'm crazy. You have to see for yourself. Will you meet me over there at midnight?" He jerked a thumb at Mr. Radzinsky's yard.

The look of curiosity on her face evaporated, replaced by an eye roll. "You want to meet outside the crazy dead guy's house at midnight? Gee, I wonder if someone's going to try to convince us the place is haunted."

He avoided her eye, flustered. "I—that is—would you just wait and see, please? Anyway, what do you mean, crazy dead guy? He was crazy?"

"Oh, yeah." Marietta folded her arms. "Total lunatic. One of those people who're, like, afraid to go out in public or talk to people."

"Agoraphobic," Spaulding said.

"A what? No, that's someone who's afraid of sweaters or something."

He sighed. "You're thinking of angoraphobic—except that's not a thing—"

Marietta gave him a withering look. "My point is, he lived there with his parents, and he never left the house, and after his parents died he stayed there alone with his giant boa constrictor. Then, if that's not crazy enough, finally that freaky snake of his ate him. And then," she concluded with great relish, "they never found the snake! It's still wandering the neighborhood, starving, bloodthirsty . . ."

"I told him that ages ago," Lucy interrupted.

Marietta scowled.

"When are you going to go in and find out for sure?" Lucy clasped her hands together eagerly

Spaulding leaned back against the side of the house. "I kind of already did. And I don't want to jump to any conclusions or anything"—he waggled his eyebrows meaningfully at Marietta—"but I witnessed some very unusual things."

Marietta's mouth fell open before she could help it. She shut it again with a snap. "Says the kid who believes in fairy tales."

"Witchcraft! I mean, I do not. Anyway, you don't have to believe me—just meet me tonight and see for yourself."

"*Pleeease*, can we?" Lucy batted her eyes at her big sister.

At that moment, the branches of the ash tree overhanging the porch rattled, as if a wind had sprung up suddenly—only the air was perfectly still. Everyone glanced around, puzzled.

And then, in a shower of brown leaves, something large and heavy fell from the tree and hit Mr. Radzinsky's roof with a thump.

Marietta and Lucy shrieked.

Spaulding barely stifled a shriek of his own, turning it into a sort of snort-cough. "Ah, yes," he said when he'd recovered. "That would be David Boa. Merely one of the unusual things I was telling you about. Perhaps you'll reconsider now?"

* * *

"This doesn't seem like a supergood idea anymore, Spaulding," a voice whispered from the darkness.

"This is by far the dumbest thing I've ever done," hissed a second voice. This one sounded both bored and furious, a difficult combination to pull off. Marietta, however, was an expert at it.

"Shh!" Spaulding flapped a hand at the shrubbery.

It was midnight, and they had just crept through the hedge into Mr. Radzinsky's overgrown yard. Spaulding had asked the Bellwoods to hide in the bushes while he knocked on Mr. Radzinsky's door. He suspected the ghost wouldn't answer if he knew anyone else was around. Although, if he was honest with himself, he wasn't entirely sure he *wanted* the ghost to show up. He was still pretty nervous about that bargain. He just hoped he could talk his way out of it if he had to.

"Mr. Radzinsky?" Spaulding called. Nothing.

The azalea bush gave a loud sigh, and Marietta stood up. "This is ridic—"

The door swung open.

Marietta gave a little yip and threw herself back into the shrubbery.

But Mr. Radzinsky was nowhere to be seen. The door might have just blown open—or maybe some ghostly power had opened it invisibly.

"Mr. R.?" Cautiously, Spaulding stuck his head inside the door. An instant later, he found himself staring at a pointy yellow-and-white face, inches from his own. A tongue whisked out and flicked the tip of his nose.

Spaulding screeched, dropped his flashlight, and fell backward down the steps, before realizing it was only David. The snake had apparently been draped over the top of the door-frame inside, either keeping watch or dozing.

Behind him, Spaulding heard stifled snorting and the rustling of azalea leaves. Drat. He could have lived without anyone seeing the shrieking-and-falling-down-the-stairs business.

"Stroke his head," Mr. Radzinsky's voice rang out. "He's offering you a rare honor!"

The snake had followed Spaulding down the stairs and was now presenting his head for patting. Spaulding gave him the quickest tap he could manage and leaned away—*somebody* had a severe case of mouse breath going on.

Above them, Mr. Radzinsky's head popped out through the windowpane. The azaleas gave a choked squawk. The ghost didn't seem to notice.

"Good evening!" he said cheerfully. "It's quite rude of you to call without advising me beforehand, but David approves, so do come in."

Spaulding got to his feet and went inside. The ghost followed right on his heels, so close Spaulding could feel a cold, clammy breeze on his back. They walked through the mudroom and into the living room.

Mr. Radzinsky floated over to what he seemed to believe was a chair, but which to Spaulding's eyes was nothing at all, and made himself comfortable in midair. "Have a seat."

Spaulding hesitated. He had a feeling Mr. Radzinsky wouldn't think it was polite if he mentioned that the room was empty, so he perched himself on nothing and tried to look relaxed.

Communing with the Spirit World

(Note: Sitting on pretend furniture
is not as easy as it seems.)

Mr. Radzinsky narrowed his eyes and looked Spaulding up and down. "You didn't bring any sort of recording device, did you? You understand this is all to be kept secret. The last thing I need is a lot of yokels realizing I'm here and coming to gawp at the phantom."

Spaulding tucked his camera deeper into his pocket. "So

you wouldn't consider letting me take some pictures or any-thing, huh?"

The ghost's skeletal hands knotted into fists. "Pictures! So you can sell them to some sleazy ghost-hunting website, or one of those idiotic television programs, I suppose?"

A faint shivering in the floorboards crept up through the soles of Spaulding's sneakers. He swallowed hard. "I just meant . . . so I don't forget anything."

"Humph! You'll simply have to take thorough notes, as any good researcher should."

"Okay, but—it's just it would be a big help for me if I could get my parents to believe me. Nobody else, just them. And if I could show them just a teeny-tiny bit of proof—" Mr. Radzin-sky shot to his feet, his face withering into an oozing death's head. All over the house, doors slammed.

Spaulding winced. "Never mind!"

The ghost lowered himself slowly back into his nonexis-tent chair. The house creaked as the pressure in the air eased. "I'm glad we have an understanding. Now . . ." He steepled his long, thin fingers in front of his face and lowered his voice. "Let us discuss the details of our . . . *agreement*."

Spaulding wiped his palms on his jeans. Here it was—the part where Mr. R demanded Spaulding go out and murder people for him, or let him leech off his life force, or something else ghastly and horrible and—

"I need you to go to the pet store," Mr. Radzinsky said.

"David Boa just loves dog biscuits, but I haven't been able to give him any for years. And his solar-powered heat lamp burned out six months ago, and I've been just at my wits' end trying to think how I'd get him a new one. Oh, and you might pick up a new bed for him, too—not fleece, it makes him itchy. Flannel will do nicely. Shouldn't you be writing this down?"

Spaulding let out the breath he'd been holding, half relieved and half irritated. If people had any idea how annoying ghosts were, nobody would go out looking for them. "*That's* what you need a living person for? *Errands?*"

Mr. Radzinsky raised his eyebrows. "I can't exactly pop down to the market myself, now can I? Don't worry, I have a bit of money squirreled away. You never know—you *might* even get a dollar or two for yourself!" He winked and chuckled.

Spaulding tried not to roll his eyes. Of course he was glad to find out he hadn't entered into a monstrous bargain with an undead creature . . . but he hadn't expected it to turn out to be quite so much like doing chores for a cranky uncle, either.

Mr. Radzinsky listed a few more errands, which Spaulding dutifully wrote down. Just as Spaulding thought he might slip into a boredom-induced coma, the ghost snapped his fingers. "I nearly forgot! There is one other thing—"

"I won't feed him!" Spaulding said quickly.

The ghost scowled. "That's not what I was going to ask. Although I must say that's not very cooperative of you. Anyway, this isn't an errand, exactly. I've had a concern on my mind recently, and I'd like your assurance that you'll help. It may never come up, but . . . if something bad ever happens in Thedgeroot, I want you to look after David Boa, and make sure he gets away safely, if it comes to that."

Spaulding frowned. "Wait a minute, what are you talking about? Do you think something bad is going to happen?"

"I don't know for certain. It's just a feeling. There's some sort of unrest in the world of the dead. It's been growing for some time, and it's centered on Thedgeroot."

"Really?" Spaulding asked, his pen racing. "Graves have been disturbed in the local cemetery—could that be it? Maybe if that's where you're buried—" Too late, he realized his mistake.

Mr. Radzinsky's eye sockets hollowed. He stretched upward, looming toward the ceiling, growing horribly thin, like a spider made of bones and shreds of skin. "I. Was. Not. Buried," he said through his teeth. "I was EATEN!"

This time, Spaulding didn't stick around to see if Mr. R. would calm down.

He leaped to his feet and ran for the door—but he'd forgotten about David. The snake was lying coiled just behind him. Spaulding tripped over the snake and stumbled a few steps, arms pinwheeling, until he crashed into the mudroom door.

It swung open, smacking into something—two some-things—on the other side. Twin yelps of surprise rang out.

Spaulding scrambled up and scurried into the mudroom to join Marietta and Lucy. Just behind him came Mr. Radzinsky and David, the snake hissing and the ghost quivering with fury.

"What is this?" Mr. Radzinsky turned his frozen yellow grin from the girls to Spaulding. "Brought your friends to see the freak show, is that it?"

"No, Mr. R—"

The roof of the small room creaked and popped. Spaulding hunched his shoulders around his ears, waiting for the ghost's rage to reach its breaking point.

Instead, he simply vanished. The door slammed.

Spaulding felt a twinge of guilt amidst the fear. He hadn't thought Mr. R would be quite that upset about having other people see him.

He looked at Lucy and Marietta, who were gaping at the house and looking nearly as gray as ghosts themselves. "Well?" he demanded.

Marietta tore her eyes away from the house long enough to notice the grin he wasn't quite able to hide.

"Fine. You win," she huffed. "Ghosts are real, you were right, blah blah blah. But you have to admit it doesn't make all the stuff you say sound any less stupid."

Chapter Eight

Note to Self: Give Team Training in Proper Stakeout Behavior

After that, it was a lot easier to convince Marietta that staking out the cemetery wouldn't be a waste of time. She was still worried about it being dangerous, but she was too curious to say no. (Lucy, of course, only had to be convinced not to go immediately.)

The three agreed to meet up at midnight again the following night. Spaulding wondered if he'd have any problem getting past Aunt Gwen this time—letting him go out in the middle of the night once was one thing, but making a habit of it might be a bit much even for her.

But as soon as he set foot in the hall at eleven-forty-five, he heard the familiar racket of snoring coming from his great-aunt's room. He didn't even have to tiptoe.

He suppressed a sigh. Every now and then, he kind of wished he had to be at least a little sneaky when he left the house late at night.

Lucy and Marietta certainly did—they were still gasping from their narrow escape when they finally arrived at the lot. Apparently their father was a light sleeper and highly vigilant about his children's whereabouts. Spaulding felt a pang of envy, even if he was a little surprised to find out their parents were divorced. One parent at home still beat zero.

"Why do you live with your aunt, anyway?" Lucy asked after he told them how easily he'd left the house. "Are your parents dead?"

Marietta gave Lucy a whack to the back of the head, but Spaulding said quickly, "It's okay—they're not dead. They're just . . . really busy. It's easier for me to live with Aunt Gwen."

The girls exchanged a shocked look, though Marietta at least tried to cover it up.

Lucy wasn't so tactful. "Your parents are too busy for you to live with them? That's totally weird."

Spaulding scowled and stomped a pinecone on the sidewalk with a satisfying crunch. "If you must know, they also think their work is too dangerous for me to be around. I don't tell people about it because it sounds like I'm bragging."

Marietta raised an eyebrow. "Bragging? Why? What do they do?"

He hesitated. He really didn't want to brag. Or humiliate himself. It was always difficult to predict which would result when this subject came up. "Well . . . they're paranormal investigators. They're on that ghost-hunter TV show—"

"Not *Peering into the Darkness: Investigations into the Inexplicable?*" Lucy demanded. He nodded.

"I love that show!" she squealed. Then she launched into a spirited rendition of the show's theme music, which was mostly just eerie whistles, beeps, and whispers.

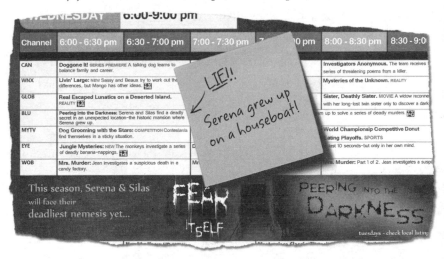

Marietta, meanwhile, did not look nearly so impressed. "Your parents are *phony TV ghost-hunters?*" she gasped. "That show—I've never seen anything so ridiculous. All they do is wander around dark rooms going, 'Did you hear that? Did you hear that?' and *you* can't hear whatever it was, and then nothing else ever happens."

She shook her head and gave him the all-too-familiar pitying look again. Clearly, this news had made her respect for him sink even lower. He'd have thought that was impossible without actually digging a hole in the ground.

He started walking again. "It's not like I'm thrilled about it, Marietta. Let's just get to the cemetery, okay?"

An awkward silence fell as they continued down the hill. It was so quiet, in fact, that when a voice rang out behind them, they all jumped a foot in the air.

"Wait up!" the voice called again.

Spaulding turned. Kenny Lin was coasting down the hill on his bike, his tires nearly silent on the smooth pavement.

"Scared you guys, huh?" Kenny asked, grinning as usual. "Whatcha doing out this late? You taking 'em to a party or something, Marietta?"

Marietta glared. "Taking Ludwig to a party? Yes, of course that's exactly what we're doing. You're *so* perceptive, Kenny."

"Hey! I *could* be going to a party," Lucy protested.

"Yeah, except Chuck E. Cheese isn't open this late."

"I'm not a baby!" Lucy wailed.

"Can we please try to focus here?" Spaulding interrupted. "We're still only a block from home. Someone could hear us and call our families."

"What *are* you doing?" Kenny demanded again. "Maybe I should call your families."

"Like you're supposed to be out at midnight," Marietta scoffed. "What are *you* doing?"

He shrugged. "I just like to ride my bike around at night sometimes. It's nice and quiet. I can think about stuff."

Spaulding blinked. He hadn't thought of Kenny as someone who'd be looking for quiet thinking time. Come to think of it, he'd kind of decided he didn't like Kenny before he'd ever even talked to him.

Kenny Lin

Friendly, funny, polite, extremely good at sports, kind, generous with French fries, blah blah blah... Why does everyone think he's so great???

To make up for being so hard on Kenny before—even though Kenny didn't know about it—Spaulding decided to be extra-nice now. "We're going to investigate the grave robberies at the cemetery," he said. "Do you want to come?"

Kenny's eyes widened. "Are you joking?"

Spaulding and Lucy shook their heads. Marietta looked embarrassed and stared off into the distance.

"That. Is. So. Cool." And before anyone could say another word, Kenny zoomed off down the street ahead of them.

"Awesome!" Lucy clapped her hands and skipped after him. "The Four Investigators, on the case!"

"Oh, gag," Marietta said.

When they neared the graveyard, Spaulding waved everyone over to a belt of trees and shrubs that edged the sidewalk. They hunkered down in the long grass.

"Now, look," he said as everyone fell silent. "This is an awful lot of people for a stakeout, so everybody has to be *really* quiet—"

"Oh, man!" Kenny elbowed him. "There's a cop car in the parking lot. This is so cool—we're staking out the same place the cops are staking out!"

Sure enough, over at the edge of the parking lot a police car lurked in the shadows.

"Shh!" Spaulding hissed. "Now it's even more important that we're qui—"

"Stupid cop!" Lucy burst out. "What if nothing happens because he's here?"

Marietta gasped. "Ludwig! What's gotten into you? It's a good thing if graves don't get robbed." She shot a glare at Spaulding. "If she ends up warped by all this, I am so holding you accountable."

"Shhh!" Spaulding flapped his hands at them. "Can we all please try to be a little more professional? If we don't keep it down, nothing's going to happen." He glanced at Marietta out of the corner of his eye. "I mean, not that we want anything to happen."

At last, everyone settled down. Seconds passed, then minutes. Spaulding glanced at his watch. It was just on the stroke of midnight. If he were superstitious, this would be the perfect time for something to—

CRACK!

Spaulding jumped. Something had made a hollow, wooden sound—kind of like a branch snapping in half, or someone kicking a door in. But nothing was stirring in the cemetery. Had he imagined it?

He looked at the others. Marietta's eyes were huge. Lucy and Kenny were clutching each other in terror.

Crreeeeak.

Spaulding and Marietta exchanged a glance. *What is that?* she mouthed.

He shook his head. *No idea.*

The sounds of muffled creaking and cracking continued. Then a thick sort of grinding, shifting noise, like a giant mouth noisily chewing, started. There was no sign of movement, but then, they couldn't see much from their hiding place.

"We have to get closer," Marietta whispered. She took the lead, picking her way cautiously through the bushes and dead grass. The others followed.

The moon was still close to full, but its light only filtered down through the trees in patches and made the shadows darker. The black wrought iron of the cemetery fence was almost invisible in the gloom. They only realized they'd reached it after Lucy walked into it with a clang. The four quickly scrambled over the low railing, Kenny giving Lucy a boost.

The giant-mouth-chewing sound was clearer now. It sounded kind of like digging, only not with a shovel. More of a gnawing, *tearing* kind of digging.

Gophers, Spaulding realized. That's what it reminded him of—like putting your ear to the ground near a tunneling gopher . . . only *big.*

Marietta suddenly dug her fingers into his arm.

"Ow," he hissed, trying to pry her fingers loose.

She ignored him, staring intently at something up ahead. He followed her gaze.

At first, all he could make out was something wriggling around in the grass in front of a tombstone. For one second, he wondered if it actually might be gophers—lots and lots of gophers . . .

Then he noticed the fingers.

A slimy, grayish hand had clawed its way out of the earth. It fumbled at the grass, trying to find a grip. More dirt welled up beside it. Another hand appeared. Slowly the arms and body that were attached to the hands—by some stringy-looking business Spaulding didn't want to look at very closely—followed them up out of the ground.

The corpse reared back its head. The mouth fell open, and a gurgling snarl erupted from its festering depths.

"I guess they can't all be like the man in the suit," Spaulding whispered.

Chapter Nine

Note to Self: No More Investigations Involving Graveyards at Midnight

"I'm gonna barf," Marietta said.

"Shh! The last thing we want is for that thing to notice us," Spaulding hissed.

The thing in question was now getting awkwardly to its feet. It pulled itself upright by the tombstone and then stood still, swaying slightly. It seemed confused (as one might expect, given the condition its head was in).

Somewhere nearby, an engine chugged to life. The sound seemed to be coming from the direction of the woods. The revenant heard it too—it paused for a moment with its head cocked, then set off unsteadily across the grass toward the sound.

"It's leaving," Kenny whispered.

"Don't relax just yet," Marietta said.

The giant-gopher noises hadn't stopped. A few feet away, the ground in front of a whole cluster of headstones was heaving up and down slightly, almost like gentle waves on a pond. Unlike gentle waves on a pond, this was followed by a collection of rotting bodies bursting forth in a shower of dirt and gravel. A smell wafted across the graveyard—a smell so foul it made the air itself seem thick and green and sticky.

Slowly, the creatures got to their feet and tottered off in the same direction as the first. Several were nothing but bones and sinew. Others could pass as living, if you didn't look too closely. A few smaller bits and pieces—fingers, toes, a nose or two—were left behind but either weren't important enough to go back for or maybe wouldn't be missed until later.

"I think we should follow them," Spaulding announced.

"I think we should go home," Lucy said in a small voice.

"I think I'm going to puke if I watch them for another second," Kenny mumbled, sinking to the ground.

Marietta hauled him to his feet. "Spaulding's right. If we don't find out where they're going, what's the use of being here at all?"

"Okay, okay." Kenny swallowed hard. "But I'm not going to look at them."

They let the creatures get a good distance ahead before following them across the cemetery and into the woods. Along with the sounds of their footfalls crunching through the leaves and branches, the rumbling of the engine continued.

"I bet I know where it's coming from," Lucy said. "Someone's driving on that dirt road we rode our bikes on. I told you it was a shortcut to town."

Spaulding chewed his lip. "But why would someone be driving out there at midnight?"

A few minutes of stumbling through thick underbrush brought them to the dirt road. The sound of the engine grew louder, almost drowning out the constant, low groans of the undead.

Lucy, who was in the lead, suddenly held up a hand. "Duck!" she hissed as she threw herself behind a clump of bushes. The others crouched down next to her. Wordlessly, she pointed through the trees.

At first Spaulding didn't see anything. But then a faint gleam of moonlight on metal caught his eye—the outline of something very large and rectangular, not more than twenty feet ahead.

"It's a truck," Kenny said, just as Spaulding realized what he was seeing. "A big truck."

The truck was idling with its headlights off, and even though it was huge, it was well camouflaged by the overgrown woods. No one was visible in the dark cab.

Spaulding shivered. There was something unsettling about the massive vehicle, so out of place on a small dirt road, its lights off and the driver unseen. All around it, the revenants milled aimlessly in a smelly, groaning crowd.

Kenny turned to him, brow wrinkled. "I don't like this, man. We're too close. If one of 'em looks over here, they'll see us. We found out where they were going, right? That's what we wanted. Now let's go, before—"

Marietta poked him. "Shh! Something's happening!"

In the truck's cab, the overhead light flicked on. The door on the far side opened, then slammed shut. Someone had gotten out of the passenger seat.

At the back of the crowd, the groans grew louder as the creatures jostled and shoved each other. They seemed to be trying to get away from whoever was approaching on the far side of the truck.

And then a slim figure in a white lab coat appeared. Even in the dim moonlight, Spaulding recognized the tense stride and the tight blond bun instantly. Dr. Darke.

The doctor strode to the back of the truck as if the revenants weren't even there. She threw open the rolling door and pressed a button to lower the loading ramp. Then she pulled a coil of something slender and rope-like from the pocket of her lab coat. She turned to face the undead creatures, who seemed to know something was about to happen. They moaned and gurgled uneasily, the crowd breaking up as they wandered off in different directions.

A few of the more energetic corpses seemed to form an idea in what passed for their heads. They massed together and shuffled back toward Dr. Darke, their hands outstretched. The awkward shambling became faster, more coordinated. The listless groans became a low, thick growling.

The doctor didn't appear concerned. With a lazy flick of her wrist, she uncoiled the object she had been holding at her side. It was a whip.

The leader of the group lunged forward, gray teeth snapping.

Dr. Darke gave her arm one quick, practiced twitch. The whip lashed out. The revenant staggered backward.

They must teach some really weird stuff in medical school.

Spaulding looked away as a new split opened in the revenant's already decaying skin. However vicious and mindless the creature was, Spaulding was still sickened to see it clutch its head and moan like an injured animal.

With a few more lashes, the doctor corralled the aggressive gang and rounded up the stragglers. Soon the crowd of corpses was in a neat line. Keeping the whip snapping expertly around their ankles, she marched them up the ramp of the truck. As the last one boarded, she lifted the ramp, yanked down the door, coiled her whip, and marched back to the passenger side of the truck.

The engine revved. In a few moments, the truck was gone. The only sign it had been there at all was a cloud of dust and a few broken branches dangling from the trees. The roar of the engine faded. The night was silent again.

Lucy finally broke the silence. "What can you do with that many dead people?" she asked no one in particular. "What *good* are they?"

Spaulding looked up from his notebook, where he was already busily scribbling notes by flashlight. "Maybe they're just cheap labor for the factory? No paid vacation, no sick days? Anyway, at least now we can all agree it's connected to Slecht-Tech." He glanced at Marietta to see how she was taking the blow.

Unsurprisingly, she was scowling. "Fine, so it's connected to Dr. Darke. I *suppose* we can assume that means Mr. Von Slecht is involved, too. But they don't manufacture anything anymore, remember? Don't tell me you think he's got them doing computer tech stuff at the corporate office."

Spaulding started gnawing his fingernails. "The smoke coming out of the factory . . . they're making something in there, I know it. We *have* to get a look inside."

"But now we can just go to the police!" Lucy said. "We know they'll find evidence if they check out the factory—the place must be crawling with revenants. We'll phone in an anonymous tip and let the cops figure out what to do."

"Hey, guys?" Kenny spoke up, scratching his head shyly. "I have no idea what you're talking about. And obviously you know about a lot of weird stuff going on that I don't know anything about. So maybe you can explain something that's really bugging me. That cop back there—he was watching for stuff going on in the cemetery, right?"

Spaulding nodded. "Yeah, so?"

"So how'd he miss a whole *gang* of dead people running around? He'd have to be blind."

Marietta frowned. "You mean he ignored it? But if he wasn't there to stop the grave robberies . . ."

The blood drained from Spaulding's face. "What if he was actually there to make sure they didn't get interrupted? We can't risk telling the police if they might be in on it."

There was a brief silence. Spaulding didn't know about the others, but he was suddenly feeling more scared than he had felt the whole time.

Then Lucy snapped her fingers. "Wait! I know—Spaulding's parents!"

Spaulding's heart sank.

"They'll believe us! And they'll know exactly what to do!" Lucy gave him a wide grin, like she expected a reward for the brilliant idea.

Kenny scratched his head. "Why would your parents know what to do?"

"They wouldn't," Spaulding muttered, heat creeping into his ears.

"Ha!" Marietta crowed. "Even you admit they're phonies? That's sad."

"I'm not saying they're phonies." He scowled at his notebook, folding the corner of a page over and over.

Lucy looked stunned. "Of course they're not phonies! How could you fake what Silas and Serena do? They're *amazing*."

"Wait." Kenny held up a hand. "You don't mean Silas and Serena Meriwether? From *Peering into the Darkness: Investigations into the Inexplicable?*"

Spaulding gave a tiny nod.

Kenny gasped. "I *love* that show!"

"Me too!" Lucy squealed. The two high-fived, then performed a duet of the theme music. Marietta scrunched up her face in disgust.

Spaulding raised his voice over the concert. "I know, I

know, everybody loves the show. But the thing is, I don't think they'd come help."

"No way!" Kenny laughed. "That's crazy. If you told 'em what was going on, of course they'd come help. You're their kid."

"You can tell them you've found a real ghost!" Lucy added. "*And* reverents!"

Spaulding cleared his throat, which was uncomfortably tight. "I already tried. They didn't believe me. They said they didn't have time to waste on one of my . . . my false alarms."

"But your notebook proves it!" Lucy said. "You write *every-thing* down—you wouldn't have made all that up."

Spaulding snorted and tossed the notebook aside. "To them, the only thing my notebook would prove is that I'm totally nuts."

There was a long silence. He didn't look up, but he could sense the others looking at each other as if they were all hoping somebody else would figure out what to say.

It was Marietta who finally spoke up. "They sound like idiots," she said briskly, "as I suspected all along. Obviously you're the smart one of the family."

He stared at her. Was she actually being *nice*? A grin spread across his face. "Well, thanks, *pal*."

Marietta looked more disgusted than she had when they'd watched corpses popping out of the ground. "All right, don't be gross about it," she snapped.

"Hang on a sec," Kenny interrupted. "Go back to the part about how you've found a real ghost?"

Marietta, Lucy, and Spaulding sighed in unison.

"Honestly, Kenny," Marietta said, "try to keep up, can't you?"

✳   ✳   ✳

Spaulding thought he might have trouble sleeping after all the excitement. In fact, he fell asleep almost as soon as his head hit the pillow.

Not long after, he found himself wide awake again. He

rolled over onto his back. Had there been some sort of noise? A thump, maybe?

He held his breath so he'd be able to hear even the faintest sound. Nothing. He was probably just jumpy because he had seen the living dead earlier—anybody would be. He rolled onto his side and tried some deep breathing.

Thump.

His eyes snapped open again. Slowly, he turned his head, trying to look as if he was moving in his sleep.

A hunched figure stood in front of the window.

Spaulding's heart started hammering. It was a revenant, come to devour his brains. Or whatever the undead did to you. Maybe the brains thing was just in movies.

Anyway, he wasn't about to give up any body parts without a fight.

"Get back, fiend!" he shrieked as he sat bolt upright and flung his pillow at the thing.

The pillow passed right through it. And then he noticed the familiar greenish glow.

He snapped on his bedside lamp and sighed. "Thanks for the heart attack, Mr. R."

Mr. Radzinsky folded his arms indignantly. David peered up over the foot of the bed, blinking in the sudden light. "I'd think you might be grateful! I came to say I accept your apology."

"Oh." Spaulding fell back onto his pillow and thought this

over. "Okay. I'm glad. And I *am* sorry. I shouldn't have used you to impress people."

The ghost sniffed and smoothed the lapels of his bathrobe. "Quite right."

"I still don't like you showing up in my room in the middle of the night, though," Spaulding added.

"Fine, fine. It's just that I saw you sneaking in late, so I thought you'd still be awake."

"What? I was so careful! How'd you see me?"

"Oh, I sit out on my roof and watch the neighborhood when my insomnia is acting up. Say, would you like to come over? The view is really quite remarkable, and I've noticed you like to sit on your roof as well."

"Now?"

"Why not? You can't sleep anyway."

He tried to protest that he had been sleeping quite well, thank you very much, but Mr. Radzinsky wouldn't take no for an answer. At last, Spaulding rolled out of bed and followed him into the hall, through the window, and out to the thinking spot.

The ghost flitted ahead to his own roof and stopped where a dormer window in the attic looked out onto a small, sloped eave. "Hurry up!" he called excitedly. "Oh, that's right—I suppose you'll have to go through the house. Well, get on with it, then. The door's unlocked."

Spaulding scooted to the edge of the porch roof and lowered himself carefully, feeling for the railing with his toes.

"Why I'm letting someone incorporeal push me around like this, I'll never know," he muttered as he dropped into the dewy grass.

David slithered ahead, looking back every now and then to be sure Spaulding was following. The snake led him through the side door and up two flights of stairs to the attic. There, the dormer window creaked slowly open, apparently of its own volition. Spaulding sighed. He was learning that Mr. R never missed a chance for some ghostly theatrics.

He swung his legs over the low sill. "This'd better be good, Mr. R. I've gotta get up early for school in the morning, and—whoa." He fell silent. The view *was* pretty remarkable.

"It's even better if you stand up," Mr. Radzinsky said proudly. "You can see for miles."

"Uh . . ." He glanced down. The ground looked awfully far away.

"Oh, fine. You can still see a lot sitting—look, there's the gas station, and the shopping center, and the baseball field. I can watch the games from here."

From this height, Spaulding realized just how tiny Thedgeroot really was—it looked like a little collection of blocks scattered in the folds of the hills. The moon was almost setting, and a heavy layer of clouds was slowly moving across the sky like a blanket being drawn up. It hung thickest over one particular part of the valley. Spaulding had a feeling it was where the factory stood.

At that moment, the clouds suddenly billowed up into a tall plume like a thunderhead or a mushroom cloud. As it sprouted, the plume flickered with a sickly yellowy-green light.

"Holy cow!" Spaulding cried. "Did you see that?"

Without even glancing over, Mr. Radzinsky's mouth turned down. "Ah, yes—it's one of the factory's busy nights."

Spaulding gasped. "You know about the factory? I thought I was the only one!"

The ghost snorted. "Oh, I know about it, all right. And mark my words, other people do, too. But no one talks about it. No one wants to cross the richest man in town. So the place just runs in secret, pouring its filth into our air and water."

Spaulding stared at him. "Is that why it's secret? So they can pollute as much as they want?"

Mr. Radzinsky shrugged. "I think so. I wrote numerous letters of complaint about it when I was alive, believe me, but it didn't do any good." He seemed to drift off in thought. Then he continued slowly, "In fact, that's my last living memory. I was sitting at my desk, writing a letter—a very scathing one, as I recall—and then it all goes dark."

Spaulding chewed his lip. This was a delicate subject. He'd have to be careful with what he said if he didn't want to make Mr. Radzinsky upset, but he had a feeling it was important that he find out more.

"I've wanted to ask you about that, sir," he said carefully.

"How exactly did anyone know what happened to you? Since there wouldn't have been a . . . you know, a *body* . . ."

Mr. Radzinsky peered at David to be sure he wasn't listening. He leaned closer. "That's a mystery I've often pondered myself," he whispered. "You see, there's a hole in my memory. The next thing I remember is waking at my desk again. But my body was gone. I knew weeks had passed because my newspapers had piled up on the porch. And I found an article about my death, so I read about what happened."

Spaulding thought this over. "But how did the reporter know what happened? Who figured it out?"

"Precisely what I wondered. The article was vague on that point—on every point, really. And I had no family or friends to look into it, so that was that. You're the only person who's ever shown any interest in what happened to me." Mr. Radzinsky smiled sadly.

Spaulding smiled back, trying not to show how depressing the whole thing was. Poor Mr. R. What a sorry life he'd had. Spaulding would have to cut him a little more slack, even when the ghost was acting like a jerk.

"Maybe somebody came by the house and found David looking, you know . . . full?"

Mr. Radzinsky frowned. "But that's the strange part, don't you see? They tried to locate him, but no one could. If they'd found him, he'd be in the pound."

The ghost looked so upset at that thought that Spaulding

decided to change the topic to something more cheerful. "Do you think I could read your letters sometime? I bet they were really good."

Mr. Radzinsky looked pleased and flustered. "Oh! My goodness! Yes, I—I suppose that would be all right. I'll get out my files for you. They're all there, except that last one. It was gone by the time I woke up, too. I suppose it's moldering in some police evidence locker somewhere." He heaved a sigh.

Spaulding fell silent. If only he could help the ghost with the puzzle of his death. But maybe at least having the chance to talk it over with someone after all this time would give him some peace.

They stayed on the roof until the clouds covered the stars. At last, Spaulding began to shiver. He wished Mr. Radzinsky and David a good night and left them there, the snake dozing and the ghost looking out at the sky.

Chapter Ten

Note to Self: Research How to Fake Own Death and Start New Life Far Away

Morning broke dreary and gray. Everything was wrapped in a thick, damp fog. Even the houses across the street were invisible. It was not the kind of day that made one feel any better about knowing the evil dead were wandering around out there somewhere. Who knew what they could be up to?

And that was just the problem—he didn't know. Spaulding didn't know much about the living dead. It wasn't the sort of thing his parents investigated, so he'd never thought he'd need any knowledge on the subject.

Which meant it was time for some serious research.

Right after breakfast, he grabbed his bike and set out. His destination was only a few blocks away—the Thedgeroot Public Library. It was a rickety old building, repurposed from its Gold Rush days as a church and hardly modernized. The steeple leaned as if it might fall off in a stiff wind, and the bell was gone. Spaulding pushed through the dark wooden doors and into a dim lobby, sunk in a dusty silence.

At the back of the reading room, an elderly man sat reading quietly in an armchair under a pair of tall arched windows. A teenage girl was slumped in front of one of the public computers, tinny music faintly audible from her headphones. Other than those two, he had the place to himself. Even the checkout desk was empty.

He did a quick search on the catalog computer—an ancient-looking machine that roared and whirred angrily at being woken from its sleep. Then he headed into the shelves, got the books he wanted, and settled at a table in a corner. He'd hardly brushed the cobwebs off the first book when a hand fell onto his shoulder.

"Spaulding Meriwether! Always so studious. It warms a teacher's heart."

Oh, great. He knew that sugary voice without even looking.

"Mrs. Welliphaunt," he said, trying to smile but not particularly succeeding. "What are you doing here? I mean, not that I'm not glad to see you." He draped an arm over his stack of books, trying to look like he was just casually leaning sideways. Mrs. Welliphaunt would definitely be the type to get all weird if she saw what he was reading.

But her teacherly instincts must have recognized the signs of a guilty student instantly. Before he could move, she snaked a hand behind his arm and whisked the whole stack away.

"What is all this? Oh, my—Necromancy: The Darkest Art? Raising the Dead and You? And—ugh—The Necronomicon?" She read the titles aloud like she'd tasted something bad, her lip curling further with every word. "Spaulding! Why ever are you reading such trash?"

Spaulding glared at her and snatched the books back. "If you must know, I have an assignment. On . . . the history of necromancy. Anyway, it's not your business—this is the public library, not the school library."

Mrs. W. has obviously been working out.

A sickly sweet smile bloomed on her face. "As it happens, Mr. Meriwether, I volunteer here at the public library. And as such"—she grabbed the books away once again—"I am fully authorized to enforce the library's rules. I am afraid your hands are simply too dirty to peruse these books. See you in class, my dear!"

She swept away without another word, every book the library had on the subject of necromancy firmly clamped under her arm. He could practically feel smugness radiating from her as he stomped out the doors in defeat.

✳ ✳ ✳

Monday morning, the moment everyone had taken their seats, Mrs. Welliphaunt rang her silver handbell. Spaulding noticed how intently she was smiling at him. His stomach tightened.

"Mr. Meriwether, would you come up front, dear? We must have a little discussion."

Spaulding forced himself to ignore the urge to bolt out the door, or fling himself out a window, or do anything at all rather than walk up to Mrs. Welliphaunt's desk.

She sighed deeply as he approached. "After I spoke with you yesterday," she said, "I took the liberty of contacting your teachers to find out who had assigned such an unpleasant and inappropriate topic." She kept her voice low, but Spaulding was sure it was only so that everyone would try even harder to listen in. The room was so quiet he could practically hear Katrina smirking.

"Imagine my surprise when I discovered you had no such assignment!" Mrs. Welliphaunt continued. "This makes me concerned for you, mein Wurstchen—very concerned. Not only does this incident reveal an unhealthy fixation on morbid topics, but it shows that you are a liar as well."

There was a rustle of surprise throughout the classroom. Spaulding could feel every eye in the room fixed on him, like tiny red-hot pinpricks in his back.

"I am not angry with you, dear. I fear for you. But never let it be said that Gretchen Welliphaunt ignores the plight of a child with a diseased mind! I've arranged help for you. Once a week, instead of going to study hall, you will go speak to the school psychologist."

There were a few gasps and stifled giggles. Katrina cackled.

Spaulding's face felt so hot he was surprised his skin hadn't melted. "This is ridiculous! I don't need to see a psychologist," he said, a little louder than he meant to.

Mrs. Welliphaunt clapped a hand to her chest. "Ach, my! Such outbursts—such rage—oh, good heavens. It is worse than I thought."

Katrina's hand shot into the air. "I've been worried about him since he got here, Mrs. Welliphaunt," she said, wide-eyed. "He talks about crazy stuff. You can ask anyone, we've all heard him."

Spaulding opened his mouth to protest again but then clamped it shut. Mrs. Welliphaunt was going to twist anything he said. He didn't know why she was out to get him, but she certainly was. If she decided to say he was having anger problems, his word would never hold up against hers. Better to stay quiet for now. The psychologist would see he wasn't the problem.

Mrs. Welliphaunt dismissed him, and he slunk back to his desk, trying not to hear the whispers and snickering all around him.

The fact that humans have not evolved the power of invisibility is an absolute DISGRACE.

After lunch, when he'd normally be heading for study hall, Spaulding lingered in the hallway, chewing his nails. Could he get away with skipping the appointment? Maybe he should go home and tell Aunt Gwen he was dropping out.

Before he could make up his mind, Mrs. Welliphaunt appeared at his locker.

"I wanted to make sure you didn't forget your appointment," she announced, giving him a sad look, like he had a terminal disease and it pained her to see him going downhill. "I know children never want to do what is best for them."

She took hold of his sleeve as if he might run away and marched him down the hall to an unmarked door. She waited until he was inside before closing it firmly behind him.

The office she'd delivered him to was nearly empty. Two chairs faced each other across a gray metal desk. A painting of frolicking puppies hung on the wall. The blinds were closed, and the light was so dim it took him a moment to register that the chair behind the desk was empty. Good. Maybe he could slip out before the counselor got back, and—

"Sit," commanded a voice. And with a loud clacking of high heels on linoleum, Dr. Darke appeared from behind him.

He sat. As she circled the desk to sit in the doctor's chair, he tried to keep his shock from showing on his face. He shot a surreptitious glance over his shoulder at where she'd been lurking, wondering what she'd been doing.

There was nothing back there. No bookcase or water cooler or anything. She'd just been *standing* there, doing nothing at all, in order to take him by surprise. What a weirdo.

"All right, boy. Speak." She folded her arms, regarding him as if he were some sort of unpleasant lab specimen rather than a patient.

"*You're* the school psychologist?" He glanced at the diploma on the wall.

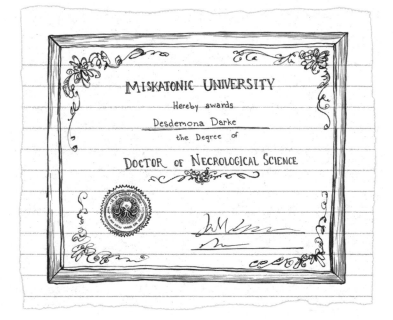

"'Necrological Science'?" he read incredulously. "That's not even a thing! How does that qualify you to be a psychologist?"

Dr. Darke opened her briefcase and took out a notepad and pen. "Subject—I mean student—displays belligerence," she commented to herself as she wrote.

"I'm not belligerent! I just—"

"Hostility. Dishonesty," she murmured as she continued jotting notes.

"Stop writing that!"

"Now, Mr. Meriwether. Why don't you tell me why you're so fascinated with death?"

"I'm not the one with a degree in 'necrological science.'"

Dr. Darke leaned back in her chair and watched him, stone-faced. "Answer the question."

He chewed the inside of his cheek. What was she up to? She wasn't the real school psychologist, he was sure of that. Had she snuck in somehow without the school authorities catching on? Or were the school authorities in on the plot, too?

But what *was* the plot? Maybe Mrs. Welliphaunt wanted the doctor to find out why he'd been researching the living dead. If that was it, there was only one excuse he could think of that might throw her off.

He cleared his throat. "The truth is, my parents are paranormal investigators. I just wanted to know more about what they do."

The doctor reached into her briefcase again and took out a manila folder labeled *Meriwether, S.*

Spaulding licked his lips. There was something very unsettling about her having a whole file about him. He wondered what else was in that briefcase of hers.

She flicked through a few pages and nodded. "Ah, yes. I see here your guardian is your great-aunt. Your parents gave you

Dr. Darke's bedside manner: not the warmest.

up, then?" She stared at him as she asked this, a faint smirk hovering on her lips.

Spaulding clenched his hands so she wouldn't see them shaking. He shrugged. "If you want to put it that way."

She pursed her lips and nodded slowly. "And so you attempt to feel closer to them by reading about this nonsensical work of theirs. Yes. I see how that could be comforting to an abandoned child."

She continued to grill him, her questions growing more and more goading. It was as if she was trying to be so mean he'd give in and admit to something—he didn't know what—just to make her stop. He tried to answer in the least suspicious, most boring ways possible. Maybe if he acted dull enough, she'd give up faster.

Eventually, Dr. Darke cut him off in the middle of a long, detailed, and horribly uninteresting story about how he'd always wanted a puppy and his parents wouldn't get him one.

"Time's up," she announced with obvious relief. "Next week—same time, same place."

Spaulding shot to his feet. *Whew*. That wasn't so bad. He could bluff his way through this once a week.

"One more thing," the doctor added.

Uh-oh.

"I have concluded that you are a danger to other students. I shall recommend to your teachers that you be moved to a desk across the room from the other students in all of your classes." She swiveled her chair away and continued scribbling in her notepad, as if he had already left the room as far as she was concerned. But he was sure he saw a little smile on her face as she turned away.

He gritted his teeth. Great. That would *really* help him fit in.

Spaulding marched out of the room without another word and then continued right out of the building. He walked all the way home in a cold, drizzling rain.

Chapter Eleven

Note to Self: Never Try to Make Friends Again

Spaulding was lying on his bed staring at the ceiling late that afternoon when the door to his room flew open. Without looking to see who it was, he pulled his pillow over his head and snapped, "That had better be the living dead, because I am not in the mood to talk to any human beings."

The mattress sank down beside him. "Dude, you're making a molehill out of a, um . . . I don't remember. Gopher hole or whatever."

"What?"

There was a loud sigh, and the mattress sagged on the opposite side. "What Kenny's trying to say is that it really isn't that big of a deal." Marietta didn't sound particularly convinced.

The mattress bounced like a trampoline as Lucy hopped aboard. "You never used to care what anybody thought of you," she said, still bouncing. "Who cares what people think? *Everybody* at my school thinks I'm weird!"

"Yeah, come on, dude!" Kenny shook his shoulder. Spaulding didn't move the pillow off his face. "Lucy's right. What happened to saying whatever you felt like, even if it sounded nuts? At least now *we* know you're not crazy. Why're you so upset?"

"This is nothing like just saying something a little unusual when I felt like it," Spaulding said from beneath the pillow. "Mrs. Welliphaunt sent me to talk to Dr. Darke, and Dr. Darke said she's going to make the whole school think there's something wrong with me."

Kenny's shoulders slumped. "Yeah, we know. Mrs. Welliphaunt went around to all your classes and made everyone rearrange the desks so yours is up front where the teachers can keep an eye on you."

Spaulding gave a muffled sigh.

"But I don't think it's gonna make anybody think you're weird or anything!" Kenny added hastily. "They'll probably think it's cool that you're so dangerous."

Spaulding peeked out from beneath the pillow. "Really?"

Kenny coughed and suddenly became very interested in his shoelaces. "Um . . . yeah!"

Spaulding clamped the pillow down again.

"Hang on," Marietta interrupted. "Dr. Darke is the school psychologist? Since when? I saw the shrink last year, after our parents split up, and it was some old guy. How'd she get the job?"

"I wondered that too." Spaulding sat up, glad to think about something less mortifying. "She didn't seem very good at it. She has a degree in something to do with studying the dead, nothing like psychology or counseling. And it all started because Mrs. Welliphaunt happens to work at the library and caught me with books on the undead."

Marietta made a face. "She's worked at the library for a while. I used to read these old history books they keep in the basement, but once she got there I wasn't allowed to see them anymore."

Spaulding's eyes narrowed. He reached for his notebook. "What kind of history books, exactly?"

She coughed and looked away. "Just stuff about Thedgeroot. Geological junk, mining . . . things like that."

Lucy rolled her eyes. "She's leaving out all the good stuff! See, this was before she started hanging with Katrina and got boring. She used to have this theory there was something weird about Thedgeroot. What was it, Marietta? Landlines?"

"Ley lines," Marietta said through gritted teeth. "They are called ley lines, and it was stupid, and shut up."

Spaulding was making notes at top speed. "There are ley lines around here?"

Lucy piped up again. "The books said so. People have thought weird stuff happened here since before there was even a town—"

Marietta cut her off. "I don't believe in that stuff anymore."

"What's a ley line?" Kenny asked. "And why would Mrs. Welliphaunt care about Marietta looking at old books?"

"Ley lines are places where there's supposed to be energy kind of flowing around," Spaulding said. "Some people believe they cause unexplained phenomena, like at the Bermuda Triangle. Or that you can harness the energy for your own use. So maybe Mrs. Welliphaunt didn't want her reading about Thedgeroot's ley lines because she's using them for something secret?"

"But I still don't get why she'd send you to counseling," Kenny said. "Why would she care about helping you?"

"She's not trying to help—that's why she didn't send him to a real counselor," Marietta said. "I think when she saw he was reading about necromancy, she got worried about how much he might know. She figures if she acts like something's wrong with him, no one will listen if he tries to tell anyone. And Dr. Darke will back her up."

"So that's it." Lucy grabbed Spaulding's pillow and hugged it to her chest tightly. "Mrs. Welliphaunt wouldn't be freaking out if she wasn't behind it all. Her and Dr. Darke."

Marietta and Kenny agreed excitedly. Spaulding knew he should be excited, too. They were finally getting somewhere— they knew who the bad guys were; they had an inkling of what the master plan might be.

But while the others talked it all over, he fell silent. He

pulled his quilt up, wrapped it tightly around his shoulders, and tried to block out the nagging fear that they were in way, way over their heads.

* * *

If he'd thought he was unpopular in school before, that was nothing compared to how things were now. Katrina was merciless every time he ran into her.

Marietta looked so uncomfortable, Spaulding almost felt sorry for her. She kept trying to pretend she didn't hear any of it, and he had the feeling she wanted to disappear almost as much as he did. Kenny would have stood up for him, but he was home sick the rest of the week. That left Spaulding entirely on his own.

After a couple of days of this, he was feeling edgy. So when a voice suddenly hissed close behind him in the hall between classes, he nearly jumped out of his skin.

"Psst! Spaulding!"

Marietta peered at him around the door of a classroom. She checked again to be sure no one else was in the hallway and then waved him over.

He raised his eyebrows. Talk about weird—Marietta wouldn't talk to him in public even before all this. Why would she be trying to get his attention now?

"Would you hurry up?" she hissed. "We don't have much time."

He followed her into the empty classroom. "Yeah?"

She shut the door behind them and leaned against it. "I've been thinking about how this all started when you saw the revenant at Blackhope Pond. That pond isn't natural—they made it back in the mining days."

He raised an eyebrow. "So? The undead don't seem interested in local history."

"Ugh! You're being stupid on purpose because you hate it

when someone else figures something out before you. You get what I'm saying—the pond is connected somehow. Maybe it's the chemicals in the water or something."

He smirked. "You're saying something in the water is waking the dead?"

She gave him a punch to the arm. "Shut up, you don't know. I'm merely examining all the possibilities, or whatever dumb thing you'd say. Anyway, I remembered this map I found in one of the books . . ."

She dug a paper out of her pocket and held it out.

He unfolded it. It was a faded photocopy of a poor reproduction of an old map, so it wasn't very clear. Still, he could make out the main landmarks. Overlaying it all was a spiderweb of faint, dotted lines.

"What are these other lines all over the place?"

"Theoretically, those are the ley lines. See where they all intersect?"

He nodded slowly. "Blackhope Pond."

"Yep. So I'm thinking—"

"Marietta?" A high-pitched voice spoke suddenly from the other side of the door.

"Oh, crap." Marietta looked around frantically for somewhere to hide, but it was too late.

The door swung open.

"There you are," Katrina said, bustling in. "I thought I heard you in here, and I—oh my God." Her eyes widened as

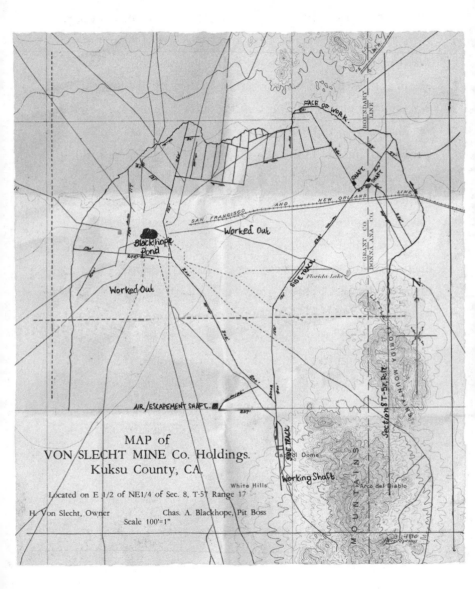

FACE OF WORK.

BOUNDARY LINE

SHAFT

SHAFT

SAN FRANCISCO AND NEW ORLEANS LINE

Worked Out

GRANT CO.

DONNA ANA CO.

SIDE TRACK

Blackhope Pond

Florida Lake

N

Worked Out

FLORIDA MOUNTAINS

Section 8 T-57 R-17

AIR/ESCAPEMENT SHAFT.

SIDE TRACK

MAP of
VON SLECHT MINE Co. Holdings.
Kuksu County, CA.

Capitol Dome

Located on E 1/2 of NE1/4 of Sec. 8, T-57 Range 17

White Hills

Working Shaft

Arco del Diablo

H. Von Slecht, Owner   Chas. A. Blackhope, Pit Boss

Scale 100'=1"

MOUNTAINS

she looked from Marietta to Spaulding and back again. A wicked smile spread slowly across her glossy lips. "What's going on in here, M? Why are you alone with Psycho Spaulding?"

Spaulding folded his arms and tried to look casual, as if he couldn't be bothered to say anything. He glanced at Marietta from the corner of his eye.

The aloof mask she always wore when she was with Katrina slammed into place. She sidled a half-step away. "I wasn't talking to him, he was talking *at* me. And wait till you hear what he told me."

He stared at her. Where was she going with this? Even she didn't seem sure—her eyes were darting around the room as if she were looking for inspiration.

Katrina didn't seem to buy it either. "Oh, please. What could this freak show have to say that would be worth being *alooone* with him for? I think there's something you're not telling me. You live near him—have you been hanging out with him?" She wiggled her eyebrows.

"Ew!" Marietta gagged—a bit too believably, Spaulding thought with annoyance. "Get real, Katrina. I don't hang around with him. My little sister does."

"Oh, sure," Katrina said, still smirking. "*That's* why you're alone with him now."

"Would you please *listen* to me?" Marietta half-wailed. "I heard him telling her the most hilarious thing. Guess why he doesn't live with his parents?"

"Hey!" Spaulding gasped. "Shut up, Marietta!"

Marietta pretended she hadn't heard him. "You know that idiotic ghost-hunting show?"

"Not *Peering into the Darkness*? I can't stand that show."

"Both of you, just shut up!" Okay, not his wittiest retort ever. But it was all he could think to say. It was useless anyway—they didn't even glance at him. The whole power-of-invisibility thing was not nearly as great as he'd thought it would be.

"That's his mom and dad." Marietta was carefully not looking at him. Which was a relief, because there was a suspicious stinging behind his eyes, and he was afraid it might show.

Katrina gasped in delight. "Oh my God! No wonder he's such a weirdo."

"Wait, there's more—they actually sent him away because they thought it was too dangerous for him to be around when they were ghost hunting!"

"No way!" Katrina shrieked. "You mean, like, they believe in ghosts? It's not just to be on TV?" She dissolved in laughter, doubled over and clutching her sides.

Marietta laughed too, shrill and loud. Spaulding finally shook off his shock enough to move and shoved past them. He caught a glimpse of Marietta's face just before the door slammed behind him. Her cheeks were fever-red and her eyes were shining, but she didn't look happy. She looked sick.

In the boys' bathroom, he locked himself in a stall. How had he been so stupid? How had he let himself think that, despite how Marietta treated him at school, underneath it she was really his friend?

He took out his notebook and flipped through it until he found the page he wanted. It took a while with his hands shaking so hard. He stared at the page for a second.

Then he tore it out and ripped it into shreds.

Chapter Twelve

Note to Self: Great Work Outwitting Dr. Darke! Yay, Me!

Spaulding didn't get out of bed in time to catch the bus the next day. Aunt Gwen would never know the difference. Anyway, she'd write a note to excuse him if he asked. Whatever Katrina was going to say about his family at school, he didn't need to be there for it.

And Marietta—she'd be right there adding details, telling everyone every stupid thing he'd ever said. She'd talk about him investigating Mr. Radzinsky's house because he thought it was haunted—and she'd conveniently forget to mention that he was right. She'd tell everyone he thought the grave robberies were the rise of the living dead, skipping the part about having seen the living dead herself.

Spaulding scooted farther under his blankets until he was in perfect darkness at the foot of his bed. There was a hiss as he squeezed his toes down into the space between the end of the mattress and the tucked-in sheet.

He let out a strangled scream. "Darn it, David Boa! Get out of there!"

The snake's head popped up. His golden eyes gleamed faintly in the gloom under the blankets. He slid forward, nudged his head under Spaulding's chin, and curled himself into a snug, contented coil that took up half the bed.

Great. He'd been asleep with a man-eating snake in his bed.

But the more Spaulding thought about it, David didn't act like a snake who would eat anyone. No wonder Mr. R. had let his guard down. In fact . . .

Spaulding threw back the blankets and sat up, frowning. Something had been bothering him about the conversation he'd had with Mr. Radzinsky the other night—something to do with David Boa and Mr. R.'s death. Spaulding had almost forgotten about it after everything else that had happened, but he knew part of that conversation didn't add up.

He snatched his notebook from the nightstand and yanked the cap of his pen off with his teeth. He had to get his thoughts organized.

Facts	Questions
1. No family, friends, regular visitors, etc.	1. Who noticed Mr. R was missing?
2. David Boa not found	2. How could they have known what happened?
3. Body not found	

He chewed the pen cap, shifting it from one corner of his mouth to the other. No matter how he looked at it, there wasn't any explanation for how anyone could have known that David ate his owner. Besides, it was awfully hard to believe it of the snake once you got to know him. He adored Mr. Radzinsky.

On the Facts side, Spaulding added,

> 4. Last known activity: writing letter.
> Location: desk.

Could it have been a heart attack? That would explain how he'd died so suddenly just sitting at his desk. He pictured it: Mr. R. slumped at his desk, lifeless. Days pass. No one notices he's missing, since no one ever saw him anyway. A growing smell drifts through the neighborhood until it can't be ignored anymore. Someone calls the police. The police arrive and find the body.

But that wasn't how it had happened—Mr. R.'s body was never found.

Okay, rewind. Body sitting there, time passing. David grows anxious—then hungry . . . too hungry to help himself?

No. As Spaulding well knew, the snake could get in and out of the house. And he'd kept himself fed all this time with no problem.

No matter how you looked at it, it always came back to the same question: Where had Mr. Radzinsky's body gone? And the answer to *that* question had to be connected to the question of how anyone had known he was dead.

Maybe the connection was that one person *had* known he was dead—the person who had killed him.

The image of Mr. Radzinsky sitting at his desk writing his angry letter floated into Spaulding's head once again—only this time, there was something new in the scene.

A shadowy figure loomed behind Mr. Radzinsky. It stepped forward, crept up silently behind him, reached out its hands . . .

Spaulding opened his eyes quickly. That was as far as he wanted to let that play.

But there was another one for the questions column:

> 3. What happened to
> the last letter?

Maybe Mr. R was right, and the letter was in a police evidence bag somewhere.

Or maybe it had been taken by the same person who had disposed of the body.

Mr. Radzinsky had said the letter had been another complaint about Slecht-Tech. What if Von Slecht and Dr. Darke had decided they couldn't let Mr. R keep drawing attention to what they were doing at the factory?

That settled it. He couldn't just lie here feeling sorry for himself. If Mr. R had really been murdered, someone had to make sure the murderers were brought to justice. And Spaulding knew just where to start looking for proof. Maybe he couldn't get inside the factory—but maybe the factory wasn't the only place where Slecht-Tech's secrets were kept.

With a quick apology to David, he swung his legs out of bed. He had a counseling appointment to get to.

* * *

Spaulding rode as fast as he could to school. He didn't have much time before his appointment, and he still had to work out a plan.

He dumped his bike in some bushes at the edge of the parking lot and slipped around to the back of the building. Cautiously, he crept along the wall, staying low and counting windows until he was pretty sure he was outside Dr. Darke's office. He peered up over the windowsill.

Jackpot. There was Dr. Darke, sitting ramrod straight at the desk, her back to the window. She was tapping away at her laptop, and her ever-present black briefcase was open beside her.

Spaulding ducked down again, chewing his thumbnail. How could he get her out of there? He considered pulling the fire alarm, but no doubt she'd grab her laptop and briefcase before she left the building. What he needed was a short distraction, something quick enough that she'd leave her things behind, knowing she was coming back soon.

His eyes fell on a wire that ran along the outside of the building and entered the wall through a hole drilled just below her office window. The phone line. What if she got a phone call, but the phone in her office wasn't working? She'd have to go take the call in the secretary's office, wouldn't she?

Carefully, Spaulding tugged the wire away from the wall. Just like everything else in the school, the phone line was old and falling apart. The brittle casing cracked as soon as he touched it, which made him feel a little less bad about damaging school property. He pulled the wire taut and sawed at it with a sharp rock until it snapped.

Then he slithered off through the shrubbery until he felt he was a safe distance away. He took out his phone and dialed the school office. "Dr. Darke, please," he said when the secretary picked up.

He was put on hold for a long time. Finally, the secretary came back on the line. "Her extension doesn't seem to be working," she said, sounding annoyed. "Perhaps I can just take a message and have her call you back later?"

"No, I must speak to her at once," Spaulding said, pitching

his voice as low as he could. "This is her business partner, Mr. Von Slecht. Tell her it's urgent she come to the phone." He held his breath and waited for the secretary to tell him to quit messing around.

"Oh, yes, sir!" the secretary said quickly. "I'll go get her, sir."

Spaulding's eyebrows crept upward. His plan was actually working. At this rate he might have to reconsider becoming a researcher when he grew up and look into secret agenting instead.

As soon as she put him on hold again, he hung up and ran to the nearest entrance, which led into the hallway where Dr. Darke's office was. He waited. A few minutes later, the secretary appeared, bustling over to Dr. Darke's door. She knocked and spoke to Dr. Darke for a moment, and then they walked off together. Dr. Darke looked concerned.

As soon as they were out of sight, Spaulding raced down the hall, his sneakers silent on the linoleum. He'd bought himself all the time he could, but he knew it wouldn't be much.

In Dr. Darke's office, her laptop was closed, but the briefcase was still open. He'd only have time to check one or the other. The laptop would probably require a password, so he went for the briefcase.

It was packed with manila file folders—she seemed to carry half of Slecht-Tech around with her. Hopefully that meant there was a good chance of finding something useful. But as he flipped through, nothing seemed unusual. In fact, everything was extremely dull. Employee files, budget files, invoices, shipping receipts . . . Everything was neatly labeled, and every folder contained exactly what the label said.

He was starting to lose hope when he noticed a single, unlabeled folder. Inside, a few newspaper clippings rested atop a stapled sheaf of perhaps twenty or thirty printed pages.

THEDGEROOT OBSERVER

etters to the Editor

Dear Editor:

Once again, I am writing to alert our community to the danger that lurks unnoticed in our quiet little town—the mysterious corporation known as Slecht-Tech Industries. Yes, despite what we are told—often within the pages of this very publication— about the benevolent local businessman and his wonderful company, I say the truth is being concealed. There is a reason the supposedly defunct factory hides behind a high fence outside of town.

Every night, from my vantage point at the top of Bracken Hill, I see things of which few other townsfolk are aware. (It is my belief that others—the police, the mayor, and other town leaders—are well aware of these secrets but turn a blind eye.) It is up to the residents of Thedgeroot to demand that the proper authorities investigate the factory and find out what Slecht-Tech is putting into our air and water.

R. Radzinsky
Thedgeroot

Spaulding stared at Mr. Radzinsky's name. There was something ominous about that red circle drawn around it like a target.

The other clippings were more of the same. Each letter described the odd noises, lights, and clouds of strange-smelling smog that Mr. Radzinsky had witnessed coming from the factory while the town slept.

Then other people began writing in response. Some defended Slecht-Tech and called Mr. Radzinsky a crackpot. But others said they believed the factory was still running. Several demanded someone be sent out to inspect the factory and enforce regulations.

Next, Spaulding picked up the stapled sheaf of papers. At first he couldn't figure out what he was reading.

```
Subject R. surveillance data   day 7


7:59 - 8:24 a.m. -- breakfast (dry toast, fried egg)

8:30 - 9:00 a.m.-- reading newspaper, muttering to self

9:10 a.m. - 12:00 p.m.-- watching People's Court

12:00 p.m. - 12:35 p.m. -- lunch

12:35 - 1:06 -
```

It wasn't until he read "6:00 to 7:30 p.m. — feeding, grooming, and talking to snake" that he understood. It was surveillance data on Mr. Radzinsky. Pages and pages of it. They'd been watching him for weeks before he died.

The file contained nothing else. No comments; no memos discussing what to do with the surveillance information; no statements issued to the paper in response to the bad publicity. It didn't really prove anything, he supposed, beyond the fact Von Slecht had ways of spying on people. It could be they'd merely kept tabs on Mr. Radzinsky and the reaction his letters received.

But as Spaulding shuffled the papers back into order, a small, tightly folded paper fell out of the stack. He picked it up. It was a different kind of paper than the rest, thick and textured. Stationery.

He unfolded it carefully.

Dear Editor:

Once again, I entreat the people of Thedgeroot to heed my warning, to demand accountability from the owners of Slecht-Tech Industries before it is too late. Only last night, I saw the factory lit up in every window, smoke pouring from every chimney, as if the very fires of Hell were being stoked within

Spaulding's heart started racing.

This was it. The last letter. And there was only one way it could have come to be here.

His stomach roiled. He folded the paper up again quickly, careful not to touch the brown stains. Just as he laid the folder back in the briefcase, he heard footsteps in the hallway—the sharp, clacking footsteps of someone wearing high heels.

Chapter Thirteen

Note to Self: DR. DARKE IS ALL-KNOWING I AM DOOMED

Spaulding started flinging folders back into the briefcase as fast as he could, but she was already almost at the door.

The footsteps stopped, the doorknob rattled—and a shrill voice rang out.

"Yoo-hoo! Desdemona, *Liebling*! I was just coming to speak to you!"

Spaulding slumped with relief. Mrs. Welliphaunt would yak at Dr. Darke for ages. He straightened up the folders and carefully shut the briefcase, then slipped into his usual seat in front of the doctor's desk.

In the hallway, Dr. Darke gave a loud sigh. "What is it, Welliphaunt? Is this regarding whatever your son was calling for? He hung up before I got to the phone, and there was no answer when I called back."

Spaulding's mouth dropped open. Her *son*? Mrs. Welliphaunt

was Von Slecht's *mother*? He shuddered. It was almost enough to make him feel sorry for Mr. Von Slecht.

"No, I haven't any idea why Werner called you," Mrs. Welliphaunt said. "Unless perhaps it was about Griselda. He *was* in a bit of a flutter about her this morning—he's convinced she's not well." A hint of irritation crept into her voice. "You know how foolish he is about that woman."

Dr. Darke snorted. "I know better than anyone."

"I was coming to speak to you about the Meriwether boy—he won't be at his appointment. He hasn't been in school today." Mrs. Welliphaunt lowered her voice. "I suspect our little plan is working. The poor dear is quite the laughingstock. I doubt he'll continue snooping, and even if he does, he certainly won't be listened to. Everyone is now well aware that he's a deeply troubled boy." She gave a dainty giggle. Spaulding clenched his fists.

Dr. Darke sniffed. "I still say my plan would have been much easier. I really can't fathom why you and Werner are so squeamish about it."

Mrs. Welliphaunt gasped. "I am a *teacher*, Desdemona! I care about young people. I would never allow harm to come to one of my dear students. Unless it was completely necessary, of course."

"Oh, what rot," Dr. Darke snapped. "As if you care any more about teaching than I do about these ridiculous counseling sessions. If that's all, I'll be getting back to the factory. I really don't know why I waste my time here at all." Still grumbling, she stomped into the office and slammed the door in Mrs. Welliphaunt's face.

Spaulding felt his palms start to sweat as Dr. Darke turned from the door. He tried to keep his voice steady. "Oh, hello, Dr. Darke. I'm here for my session. I had to miss morning classes for a—um, a doctor's appointment, but I'm back now."

Dr. Darke didn't reply. Her razor-sharp gaze slid from his face to the closed briefcase.

Oops. It had been open when he came in.

"Spying again, were we?" Dr. Darke said.

She crossed to her desk and leaned on the edge of it in front of him. Spaulding gripped the arms of his chair nervously. But the doctor merely picked up a nail file and examined her perfectly polished fingernails. She gave the edge of one a few delicate swipes with the file.

"You fancy yourself quite the little detective, don't you? If I actually wanted to *counsel* you"—she curled her lip at the thought—"I'd tell you to stop trying to impress your parents. They obviously don't care what you do."

Before he could respond, she tossed the file aside, leaned down toward him, and seized his jaw in an iron grip. She tilted his face from side to side, scrutinizing him. Her red fingernails dug painfully into his skin. He thought she'd look angry, but instead she was smiling. And somehow that was much, much worse.

After what seemed a very long time, she leaned in until her face was so close he could feel her icy breath. He tried to lean back, but her fingers tightened until his jaw creaked.

"And if you're still tempted to snoop," she said, "just keep in mind—*I am watching you.*" She shoved him away, hard, and strolled over to her own chair.

"I don't know what you're talking about," he said shakily.

"You and Mrs. Welliphaunt are the ones who told me I needed counseling. I'm just doing what I thought I was supposed to."

The doctor stared at him, her eyes as cold and flat as two dimes. "You're obviously beyond help. Your sessions are over. And the next time I catch you snooping, you will not get away from me alive. Now get out."

He got out.

His heart was pounding and his hands were shaking as he stepped outside. He'd gotten information, all right. But Dr. Darke knew. She knew *everything*. And he had no doubt she was ruthless enough to do exactly what she'd threatened.

Yet as he hurried across the parking lot to his bike, a little of the tension drained away. He'd gone right into the lion's den and come out unscathed. He scratched at his jaw as a small smile crept across his face. Katrina thought *she* was intimidating? She'd crumble if she ever faced Dr. Darke the way he just had.

Just then, the sun came out from behind a cloud and gilded the school buildings and the bare trees. It wasn't as warm as it looked, but he turned his face toward it, breathing easier with every step.

His jaw itched again. It felt like an insect was crawling on him. He paused to check his reflection in the side mirror of a car—and gasped in shock.

A row of deep, blood-red crescents scored his skin, four on one side and one on the other.

He angled his head to see them better, rubbing gingerly at his skin. He forgot all about the odd little itch. And he didn't notice that right where the itch had been—just above the fingernail gouges—a tiny, silvery speck glistened in the momentary ray of sunlight.

Then the sun went back behind the clouds, and the speck turned nearly invisible again as it wriggled its way up toward his ear and deeper into hiding.

* * *

The moment homeroom was over on Monday morning, Kenny ambushed Spaulding at his classroom door.

"I've been waiting to talk to you forever! Why weren't you in school on Friday? Why were you invisible all weekend? I came by your house like a million times but no one ever answered the door."

Spaulding sidestepped him and kept walking toward his locker. "I had homework to catch up on."

"Yeah, right. You finish all your homework before school even gets out for the day. Something happened while I was out sick, didn't it? Katrina knows all about your parents now, for one thing. Were you trying to impress her or something? 'Cause it definitely did not work."

That was for sure. She'd spent all of homeroom with her phone out, making everyone watch the most embarrassing clips from *Peering into the Darkness* she could find. (Mrs. Welliphaunt had suddenly and conveniently become blind to students goofing off.) And Spaulding had an inkling that the hilarious new nickname for the show everyone was using— *Peeing into the Darkness*—was Katrina's doing as well.

He stifled a sigh. "Marietta told her."

Kenny gasped. "No! That's too low, even for Marietta. Are you sure? Maybe she just found out somehow."

"I'm sure. And I'd rather not talk about it, thank you."

"Dude, don't take it out on me. You're, like, shutting me out because *they're* jerks. I didn't do anything."

Spaulding edged away. "Look, it's only a minute till the bell rings. We'll talk some other time."

Kenny raised his eyebrows. "*Some other time?* What's that supposed to mean? How about, like, the second school gets out, *duh?*"

"I don't know. I might not be home."

The bell rang, saving him from further awkwardness. He hurried away, pretending not to notice Kenny still standing there staring at him.

*　*　*

Spaulding chewed his nails all through history class, not hearing a word of Mr. Robards's lecture. He felt bad about what had happened with Kenny, but he couldn't let himself soften.

No matter how nice Kenny acted, what happened with Marietta had opened Spaulding's eyes. Sure, his plan had worked, and he'd convinced some kids to spend time with him because they were interested in the mystery he'd uncovered. But he hadn't made *real* friends. They only cared about the revenants and the ghost and the haunted serpent. They didn't care about him. Well, now he knew better. From this minute on, he was in it alone, as he should have been all along.

All he had to do was find concrete proof there was black magic going on in the factory. Once he revealed that to his parents, they'd take him back, and he'd move away from this town forever.

The sound of muffled snickering broke into his thoughts. He jerked his head up to find Mr. Robards sneering at him.

"Well, Mr. Meriwether?"

"I'm sorry?"

"Oh, goodness no! I'm sorry our poor little history class is too dull to hold your attention. Since you aren't interested in responding to my question, perhaps there's a topic you would rather address—red mercury, or black magic, or . . . . or . . . the bogeyman, perhaps!" Mr. Robards was so indignant he was sputtering.

Spaulding sighed. "No, Mr. Robards. I'll pay attention now, sir."

The history teacher resumed the lesson, though he continued to shoot Spaulding frequent dark looks. Spaulding tried his best to appear attentive—but his mind was buzzing again, and not with thoughts about history class.

Red mercury.

He couldn't believe he hadn't thought of it sooner. When he'd brought it up to Mr. Robards before, he hadn't taken it seriously; he'd just thought it was an interesting bit of folklore. But compared to ghosts and the rise of the living dead, the existence of red mercury no longer seemed like such a stretch.

It fit with what Marietta had said about Blackhope Pond. The pond was artificial, a by-product of mining, and full of mercury. She'd also said all the ley lines intersected there. Red mercury was supposed to be formed when regular mercury underwent an alchemical transformation. What if the pollution in the pond combined with the energy from the ley lines was creating red mercury? That would explain why his cell phone went haywire there; electronics were supposed to be affected by red mercury.

It would explain something else, too. Red mercury was extremely rare—so rare most people would say it didn't even exist—and that, combined with the powers it was supposed to have, made it very valuable.

Valuable enough to interest a powerful businessman. Valuable enough that someone might have an entire business built on secretly collecting it.

✳   ✳   ✳

Spaulding's teeth clacked against each other as his bike bounced down the old gravel road leading to Blackhope Pond. The moment he'd gotten home from school, he'd grabbed his bike and left. (He did stop in the kitchen, despite feeling ridiculous, to pour a handful of salt in his pocket. Lately, some of his parents' ideas didn't seem so stupid.)

He made sure he was gone before Kenny showed up. He didn't want to talk things over or listen to Kenny try to pretend they were really friends. It was easier this way.

At the clearing, the pond was as black and silent as ever. He scanned the woods carefully for anyone hiding there, undead or otherwise, but nothing moved. The only sound was leaves crunching under his feet.

He pulled out his phone. It didn't have any reception, but that was normal for being this far out of town. Since he was close to where it had acted peculiarly before, he decided to keep it out and watch it for any strange activity. He held it in front of himself and kept one eye on it as he walked even though it made him feel like an extra on Star Trek exploring an alien planet and waving a tricorder around. Thank goodness no one could see him.

But as he thought this, the feeling of being watched crept over him.

At the same instant, his cell phone blared a discordant ring tone he'd never heard before. Spaulding flinched, and the phone slipped out of his hands. It landed faceup, the screen blank. No incoming call. The ringing switched abruptly to vibrate and then stopped altogether.

He wiped his palms on his jeans and retrieved the now-silent phone. So it hadn't been a fluke when it had acted weirdly before. That must mean he was getting close to—

Snap!

A branch broke nearby. He spun around, heart pounding.

A little distance away, a sheepish face peered out of the bushes.

"Hey," Lucy said with a feeble wave.

"Jeez, Lucy." Spaulding slumped over and put his hands on his knees. "For the last time, *quit doing that!*"

She stuck her lip out. "But I wanted to make sure you were okay! I saw you leaving all by yourself, and I was worried."

"You came out here just to see if I was all right?"

"Sure. I tried to get Marietta to come too, but she was acting all weird for some reason. Sorry it's just me."

"No—I'm glad it's just you."

Lucy's face lit up. "You *are?*" She burst out of the bushes and ran over to throw her arms around him. Daphne's case slammed into the back of his knees as he gave Lucy an awkward pat on the back.

Lucy pulled away and glanced around. Her smile wavered. "But, um . . . isn't it kind of . . . *dangerous* out here?"

Spaulding's heart sank. Just because it was a relief for him to have company didn't mean he could put Lucy in danger.

"You're right. You have to go home. I can't let you be out here."

Lucy's mouth fell open. "Let me? Let me? You're as bad as Marietta—ever since our parents divorced, she thinks she has to protect me from everything. But at least she has the right to boss me around. She's my sister! You can't tell me what to do."

"I'm not bossing you around, Lucy. I just don't want anything to happen to you because of me."

"It isn't 'cause of you—I'm making up my own mind. This way, we can look out for each other while we . . . um, what are we doing out here again?"

Quickly, he filled her in on his theory about the red mercury.

Lucy pushed her glasses up her nose and looked doubtfully at his phone. "I don't get it. What's the point of this red mercury stuff, even if it is here? What's it do besides mess up phones?"

"Well, the folklore says it can do everything from curing illness to turning common metals into gold to giving power over the dead. I think Von Slecht is collecting it from the pond. I was hoping there might be some kind of evidence out here, but so far there's nothing."

Suddenly, Lucy grabbed his sleeve. "Wait—what's that?"

She was pointing to a large, corrugated metal drainage tunnel that stuck out of the bank of the pond. A stream of dirty-looking water trickled out of it, carrying bits and pieces of trash along with it. One particularly large piece seemed to have caught Lucy's eye. Spaulding couldn't see it well from this distance, but it appeared to be a grayish-white stick.

"It's just a piece of litter," he said. But he pushed his way through the tangled shrubbery overhanging the bank to get a clearer view.

Suddenly, the soft bank gave way beneath him. His foot plunged down and splashed into the pond. He managed to cling to a few skinny branches to keep himself from falling all the way in, but he still ended up with both feet ankle-deep in scummy water. On the bright side, he got a good close look at the stick—and then kind of wished he hadn't.

Thedgeroot has a SERIOUS pollution problem.

Chapter Fourteen

Note to Self: Wash Feet with Disinfectant Tonight

"Can you see what it is?" Lucy called down to him.

"Yeah," he called back. "It's an arm."

"Ewww!" Lucy screeched. "Lemme see." The shrubbery thrashed around wildly. Eventually Lucy's head popped out, her hair now looking quite a lot like a birds' nest. She peered down at the arm. Then she glanced around at the gloomy woods. "Um . . . does this mean there's a relevant wandering around here looking for that?"

Spaulding chewed his lip. "It came down through that big drain tunnel, so I guess the rest of it must be upstream somewhere."

They were silent for a moment, staring at the arm bobbing in the water.

Suddenly, Lucy gasped and sat bolt upright. "Wait! If they've been taking all the dead people to the factory . . . and

part of a dead person got here through that drain tunnel . . .
doesn't that mean the tunnel probably connects to the factory?"

Spaulding thought this over for a second. Then a smile
broke across his face. "And that means the tunnel goes under
the fence. I know we'll find something at the factory, and now
we've finally found a way in."

He looked back at the culvert, and his smile faded. A worm
of fear writhed in the pit of his stomach. The tunnel—that
gaping, dripping, pitch-dark mouth—that was their road into
the factory.

Enclosed dark spaces were not Spaulding's thing. Especially not enclosed dark spaces that were full of scummy greenish-brown water that had dead-people-parts in it.

Lucy peered into the mouth of the culvert. "It's not that bad." She took a step in, her voice echoing hollowly. "You can almost stand up straight and everything."

"All right, come on, Spaulding," he muttered to himself, wiping his palms on his jacket. A raindrop splatted onto his head. "It's just a short pitch-black tunnel that could collapse on you at any moment. It's not even that deep underground. You'd be able to claw your way out of the rubble eventually, as long as you weren't crushed or suffocated first—"

"Would you stop that!" Lucy yelled from somewhere ahead.

The rain began to fall faster, trickling under his collar as the wind gusted. He took a deep breath and waded forward.

A few feet in, the last bit of daylight was swallowed up in total darkness. But as always, his trusty flashlight was in his backpack. A moment later, its friendly white beam cut a swath through the black. The tunnel walls stopped pressing in on him.

Spaulding aimed the light so he and Lucy could both see. Every few steps he flashed it ahead to make sure nothing unexpected awaited them. Besides the sounds of their feet sloshing and the occasional drip from the ceiling, the tunnel was silent. The air was cold and moldy-smelling.

Spaulding tried to put himself in a sort of trance—left foot, right foot . . . breathe in, breathe out . . . don't start imagining what might be about to brush up against you . . . left foot, right foot . . .

Somewhere along the line, the culvert had gotten much wider and taller. It was no longer a corrugated metal tube, but an earth-walled tunnel. He wondered if they had entered an actual mine shaft. At least now it smelled more like cold dirt than mold, and the air circulated more freely—but if they had entered the system of mine tunnels, that meant they could get lost.

"Look!" Lucy whispered suddenly. She pointed ahead. "No, don't shine the light up there—then you can't see. It's daylight!"

She was right. Not far ahead, a faint white glow outlined the tunnel walls. They rushed onward and turned a corner to find themselves at the lip of another short length of corrugated metal tunnel. Pale sunlight filtered through a grating at the end.

Spaulding pressed his face to the grate and tried to see out, but could only make out a few feet of a shallow ditch.

"We're not stuck, are we?" Lucy asked.

"No, I can get my arm between the bars—I just hope no one's watching." Stretching his arm as far as he could, he could just reach the rusty latch on the outside of the grating.

The grate creaked open, and he stuck his head out

cautiously. They were at the edge of a field. Before him, the drainage ditch continued for another ten or fifteen feet before disappearing into a veil of rain—the scattered raindrops had become a downpour while they were underground. Further off, the outline of several large rectangular shapes loomed.

"Slecht-Tech," Lucy whispered.

They scrambled out of the tunnel and up the bank of the ditch, heading toward the ghostly silhouette. Gradually, the smokestacks appeared through the mist. Smoke billowed above them—the factory was running.

The ditch led to the wall of the largest building, where several pipes protruded over the water.

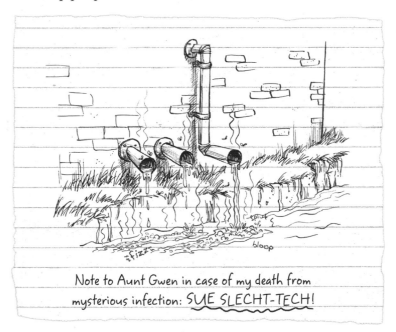

Note to Aunt Gwen in case of my death from mysterious infection: SUE SLECHT-TECH!

Lucy plugged her nose. "Ugh, it stinks! What is that?"

"Shh!" Spaulding grabbed her wrist and pulled her down into the tall grass.

At the edge of a small courtyard in a corner of the main building, a door opened. Dr. Darke emerged, speaking into a cell phone. She looked annoyed.

"I still say you're overreacting, Werner," she said, striding briskly across the courtyard. "I'm sure there's nothing wrong with her." She paused, listening, then gave an angry snort. "Yes, yes, I'll be there in a moment. It isn't as if I have any actual work to do, after all." She hung up the phone and disappeared around a corner, her footfalls echoing across the featureless cement walls.

"Quick," Spaulding whispered. "Let's see if she left that door unlocked."

They scrambled through the tall grass to the cracked pavement of the courtyard. Luckily, the only windows facing them were boarded up, so there was no fear that anyone would see them. The door was not only unlocked, but ajar. Spaulding peered through the crack to make sure it was empty and then slipped inside, Lucy on his heels.

They found themselves in a laboratory. Gleaming steel tables held all kinds of scientific equipment—computer monitors, microscopes, racks of test tubes, Bunsen burners. Rows of white cabinets lined the walls.

Lucy picked up a jar from the nearest table and read the

label. "*Preservative formula #31.*" She made a face. "Preservatives? Yawn! I thought it would be eye of newt or frog's breath or something. Does that mean Slecht-Tech just does, like, food science?"

Spaulding glanced at the jar. "I'm guessing it's the workers that need preserving." He began working his way down the rows of cabinets, peering into each one. "Look at this." He pulled out a large, unlabeled metal canister. A fine red grit coated the rim. "I think that's red mercury. There are tons of these canisters in the cabinets."

Lucy moved on to inspect a bookshelf in the corner. "*Whoa*—check this out. Is it some kind of really old science book?" She held a thick, dusty volume out for his inspection.

Carefully, he turned the crumbling pages. "I don't think that's about science. Those symbols are runes. And the title of this drawing here . . ." He pointed at an engraving that depicted a man crouched over a prone figure that appeared to be either sleeping or dead. "Nekro . . . something something . . . logos. That's something about 'language of the dead' in Greek. I think this is a spell book."

He started to read more closely, but Lucy grabbed his wrist. "We don't have time! She might come back any second."

Spaulding chewed his thumbnail, weighing the book in his other hand. A real spell book. One that apparently worked. If he showed his parents this, they'd have to listen to him.

"Come on, Spaulding," Lucy whispered. She opened the door a crack and peeked out.

While her back was turned, Spaulding made up his mind. He shoved the book under his T-shirt and his bulky sweatshirt, the leather binding warm against his skin. If he kept his arm tight against his side, you couldn't even tell it was there. Lucy would make a fuss about it if she knew, and he didn't want to argue. It wasn't going to hurt anything to take it, he told himself. It was for research.

Ignoring the little alarm bell going off in the back of his mind, he ran after Lucy.

❋ ❋ ❋

"Where to next?" Lucy asked, keeping her voice low.

Spaulding glanced around. The direction Dr. Darke had

gone was out, obviously. That left one other choice: a rusty door in the building across from the lab.

The door opened into a long, dim room. The only light came from cracks around the boards that covered the small windows high above. Ancient, hulking machinery, blanketed with rotting tarps, filled the space. Clearly, this part of the factory really was abandoned and had been for a very long time.

Lucy tugged on his sleeve and pointed at a set of metal doors in a corner behind a pile of broken mine carts. "That looks like an elevator," she whispered. "Do you think it still works?"

The control panel next to the doors had only one button— down. Spaulding pressed it, not expecting anything to happen. But instantly there was a bone-shaking clamor of machinery grinding to life in the walls. The doors screeched open.

"I'm not riding in that thing," Lucy said, staring into the tiny metal box. "You shouldn't either. It looks like it'll fall apart if you breathe on it too hard."

"Okay, you wait here, then. If anyone comes along while I'm gone, just hide until I come back."

Without waiting for her to argue, Spaulding stepped into the elevator and pressed the down button. The elevator sank slowly, shaking and clanking all the way. At last, it ground to a halt and the doors rolled back.

Spaulding stepped out onto a metal catwalk overlooking a cavernous, windowless room. It was crowded with people and echoing with the noise of machinery. Quickly, he ducked behind the railing of the catwalk. After a few seconds, when no one raised an alarm, he risked a peek over the edge. His eyes widened.

"I guess I found the revenants," he muttered.

The place was full of them. They shuffled around carrying boxes; they pushed buttons and pulled levers and loaded crates. It wasn't too different from any manufacturing plant, except that no one spoke or looked at each other or stopped their tasks even for an instant.

At one end of the room, a row of empty metal canisters, the same kind they'd seen in the laboratory, moved down a conveyor belt. As they passed under the mouth of a large funnel, a stream of dark red powder gushed out and filled each canister. Then a mechanical arm clamped a cover on, and a revenant stowed the filled canisters in a crate.

As Spaulding watched the revenants slaving away, he was startled to find he recognized one relatively well-preserved specimen shuffling along with a crate of canisters in its arms. One hand was missing a few fingers.

Spaulding felt oddly pleased to see the old guy. He must have wandered out of the factory that day they'd seen him in the woods. Maybe he'd been trying to escape. Maybe he'd done it more than once, too, and that was how he'd ended up at the pond the first time Spaulding had seen him.

It was kind of sad, now that he thought about it. Maybe

The man in the suit:
still ~~alive~~ not dead!

somewhere deep down, all the revenants longed for the peace of the grave. They certainly didn't *sound* very happy—as they worked, they groaned and sighed continuously.

And what was the point of all their work, anyway? Was Von Slecht really raising the dead just to make red mercury, which he then used to . . . raise the dead? There had to be more to it.

Spaulding stepped back into the elevator. There was one more button—B2. A sub-basement.

The elevator seemed to travel down a lot longer this time. When the doors finally opened again, the first thing Spaulding noticed was the smell of cold earth. He was deep underground now. The roof of the cavern was far overhead, lost in the dark. And it *was* a cavern, not a building. The walls and floor were jagged stone.

Everywhere Spaulding looked, hundreds of revenants were digging, swinging pickaxes, and even driving bulldozers as they carved out tunnels branching off in every direction. It reminded Spaulding of an enormous ant farm—except he kind of liked ants.

Spaulding swallowed hard. He thought he'd gotten used to the undead, but seeing this many was making his stomach tie itself in a knot. It wasn't just the smell or the sight of the occasional head suddenly falling off its owner. It was the realization that whatever Von Slecht was up to, it was bigger than Spaulding had ever suspected.

At this point, really starting to question whether we're equipped to handle this situation.

* * *

Lucy was hiding under an ore cart when he got back upstairs. The instant he stepped off the elevator, she burst out of her hiding place and rushed him.

"There you are!" She grabbed his sleeve and hauled him to the door they'd come in by. "What took you so long? What did you find out?"

Spaulding thought about the cavern and shivered. "I'll tell you about it once we're outside. Right now, I just want to get as far away from here as possible."

After the noise of the cavern, the aboveground parts of the factory seemed eerily quiet. They crept along the edge of the main building, keeping close to the walls, and were almost back to the courtyard when the sound of a door slamming nearby made them freeze in their tracks.

"Would you please stop fretting, Werner?" Dr. Darke snapped. "Griselda is *fine*. Or at least, as fine as she ever is. You won't help anything by mooning around the lab while I look at her."

Spaulding and Lucy managed to duck behind a Dumpster just before Dr. Darke and Mr. Von Slecht came around the corner. Von Slecht was escorting a woman who Spaulding figured must be his wife. She was extremely pale, with wavy dark hair and an elegant black dress, like some glamorous old-time movie star who'd stepped right out of a black-and-white film without getting colorized. She didn't say a word as Von Slecht herded her along ahead of him.

"I didn't ask for your opinion," Von Slecht said. "Just do your job. Treat my wife."

Dr. Darke snarled something under her breath as she held the laboratory door open for Von Slecht and his wife to enter.

Spaulding's breathing slowed a little. If they hadn't been so distracted by squabbling, he was sure they would have sensed they were being spied on. As it was, they disappeared into the lab without even looking around. The door slammed behind them.

"*Whew*," Spaulding breathed. "Let's get out of here."

They raced off into the long grass of the field toward the drain tunnel.

If they had stayed a moment or two longer, they would have heard a commotion inside the lab. There was a crashing and banging of things being thrown around in a frenzy, and a voice sliced through the silence of the factory.

"Where is my book? I left it right here. It's not here—*it's not here!*"

The lab door was flung open and smashed into the wall. Dr. Darke stepped out, her face tight with fury. Her sharp eyes scanned the darkening field, where a flattened trail of grass showed the direction Spaulding and Lucy had gone as plainly as a pointing finger. A tiny smile crept across Dr. Darke's thin lips.

"Werner," she said over her shoulder, "unlock the cells. I'm going to need a team of our less *friendly* specimens."

* * *

By the time Spaulding got home, he felt like he'd been gone for ages. In fact, it was only a little after dinnertime, but he went straight to bed anyway. He'd never been so tired. He only hoped his worries about what they'd found at the factory wouldn't keep him awake.

They didn't. He fell into a deep sleep as soon as he closed his eyes. When he woke, he couldn't remember having a single dream to bother him all night long—although, he realized groggily, he hadn't made it through the night yet. It was still pitch black in his room.

The back of his neck tingled. Something had woken him from a sound sleep. Someone was in the room.

He held his breath and lay very still. The floor behind him gave a tiny creak. And then he realized this all felt very familiar.

He flipped over with a sigh. "Mr. Radzinsky, I told you I didn't like you coming in unannounced—"

But it wasn't Mr. Radzinsky.

So completely SICK of waking up
to dead people in my room
(and I refuse to even think about what that puddle is).

Chapter Fifteen

Note to Self: Who Knew One Little Souvenir Would Turn into a Big Hairy Deal?

The revenant swayed a little, its bones grinding faintly as it moved. From its throat came a low growl.

Spaulding felt a ripple of terror like ice water down his back. *Growling?* That was new. It didn't seem good.

He scooted across the bed so fast he fell out the other side, stumbled to his feet, and dashed for the door.

The creature snatched at him as he passed. Leathery fingers wrapped around his arm.

Spaulding wrenched hard against its grip. The revenant held on tighter—but the strain was too much for its decomposing hand. With a wet *shlurp*, Spaulding's arm slipped free.

He shuddered, holding his damp arm away from himself. "I'm going to have to disinfect everything in this whole room," he muttered.

As he opened the door, a whiff of rot hit his nostrils and a chorus of moans and groans arose from the hallway. Great—more of them. It was dark in the hall, but from what he could see, it was pretty crowded.

Behind him, the revenant in his room sidled closer, clacking its finger bones greedily.

He was trapped.

An angry hissing broke out in the hall. Underlying the stench of death, Spaulding caught the familiar scent of rodents and alligator handbags. Then a long, heavy form swooped down from above, sending the undead flying like bowling pins.

"David Boa!" Spaulding cried.

The boa constrictor had apparently been sleeping on top of the bookshelf in the hall, and he didn't seem too pleased that his nap had been interrupted. Within seconds, he had the revenants in the hall hopelessly entangled. The one in Spaulding's room tried to make a break for it, but the snake sank his teeth into the creature's leg and dragged it to the ground with the others.

While David busied himself with squeezing his victims, Spaulding edged past, heading for Aunt Gwen's room. "Thanks!" he called over his shoulder. The snake gave a self-satisfied flick of his tongue.

Spaulding wasn't sure exactly what he was going to tell her—*Hey, Aunt Gwen, sorry I didn't mention this before, but I'm being stalked by the dead?*—but it was clear he had to tell her something. If revenants were going to be attacking them in their own home, it was just too dangerous to keep her in the dark any longer.

"Aunt Gwen! Wake up!" He lifted a fist to bang on her door, but it swung open at the first touch.

His heart began to pound. He flicked on the light. It cast a warm glow over the rumpled, empty bed.

"Aunt Gwen?" he whispered.

Across the room, the curtains stirred in a breeze from the open window. But Aunt Gwendolyn was always cold. She never left her window open at night.

Slowly, Spaulding crossed the room and looked out. The yard below was empty. The street was silent.

"Aunt Gwen . . ." he repeated hopelessly.

* * *

Spaulding wasn't sure how long he'd been standing at the window, his mind blank, before the silence was broken by the sound of bare feet on pavement. Marietta and Lucy raced up the street.

"Spaulding!" Marietta waved frantically. Lucy was silent, her face streaked with tears.

"I'm coming!" he yelled.

Back in the hall, there was no sign of David or his captives—he must have dragged them off somewhere to dispose of them in private.

Note: Artist's rendition — actual events may have occurred slightly differently.

Outside, Lucy sobbed as Spaulding ran up. "They took our dad, Spaulding!" She clutched Daphne to her chest tightly. "What are we going to do? Why would they take him?"

"They took Aunt Gwen, too." He realized he was shivering, both from the cold—he was only wearing his pajamas—and from sheer panic.

"What about Kenny?" Lucy sniffed.

Spaulding's heart sank. She was right. Poor Kenny was mixed up in this, too. "We have to go check on him."

But Marietta shook her head. "No. This has gone way too far. We have to go straight to the police."

"And tell them what?" Spaulding wrapped his arms around himself against the chilly air. "We've been over this. They'll never listen."

"But now they'd have to listen! There's hard evidence—our families are missing."

"Yeah, and how do we get them to believe that we know where they are? We say the undead kidnapped them and we know who the necromancer is? That'll be really convincing. Look, we don't have time to argue about this. We need to get to Kenny's house, fast. Then we can figure out what to do next."

Marietta scowled, but she didn't argue anymore. She and Lucy went back to their house to get their bikes and slip on sneakers, and Spaulding did the same. While he was in his room, he grabbed his backpack and threw in his flashlight, notebook, and anything else that seemed as if it might come in handy.

A few minutes later, they met up again in front of Spaulding's house. There was a brief delay while they discussed whether Lucy could bring Daphne, but at last, they were ready to go.

As Spaulding mounted his

Expressed concern re: Daphne slowing us down.

But Lucy made a convincing case for bringing her.

bike, an imperious voice rang out behind him. "Just a moment there!"

He turned to see Mr. Radzinsky glaring at him, his head thrust through the wall of his house. Marietta flinched at the sight of him, and Lucy cowered behind Daphne.

The ghost eyed the girls a little guiltily. "Hello again, you two. No need to be alarmed."

"But you don't want us to see you!" Lucy squeaked from behind her instrument case.

Mr. Radzinsky harrumphed and smoothed his hair. "Ah, yes. I suppose I *was* a bit touchy about that the last time we met. But I've turned over a new leaf. I'm trying to get out more, make new friends—being dead is no reason not to have a social life, eh? *Heh!*"

The girls laughed nervously at Mr. Radzinsky's little joke and edged farther away as soon as he wasn't looking.

The ghost turned to Spaulding. "Now, Spaulding, where is David? He went to your house over an hour ago."

"Yeah, I saw him. Actually, he saved my life. A bunch of revenants tried to kill me, but he protected me."

Mr. Radzinsky couldn't hide a smile. "Well! I'm not surprised. He *is* very assertive. But if you see him again, send him home directly."

Spaulding nodded and turned away.

"Hold on there." The ghost leaned farther out of his wall, squinting. "What is that peculiar *aura* around you?"

Spaulding looked down at himself. T-shirt, striped pj pants, feet . . . nothing seemed to have an aura.

"I can't quite make it out from here . . ." Mr. Radzinsky waved him closer. "Ah, yes, that's it—there's a bug on you."

"What? Ew! Get it off! Get it off!" Spaulding squealed, slapping at his hair and pajamas.

The ghost somehow managed to roll his eye sockets. "Not *that* kind of bug. Someone's watching you." He crooked his finger for Marietta to come closer. "Look at his head, right there. You see it?"

Marietta leaned forward to look closer. "Oh, gross—there is something . . ."

Spaulding felt her tug at his hair just above his ear. Then she held something out on her fingertip for him to see. It didn't look like much more than a whitish speck until he took it from her and brought it right up to his eye.

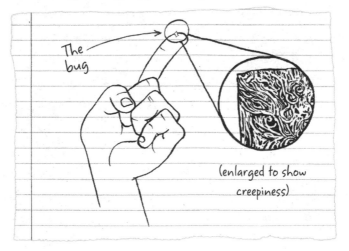

The bug

(enlarged to show creepiness)

"Is it electronic or something?" he asked Mr. Radzinsky.

"Heavens, no. It reeks of black magic. You've heard of spells that use part of a person—hair or fingernail clippings or some such—to put a hex on them? This is similar, except in this case the spell uses a part of the spell-caster, not the victim. It's made of someone's skin."

"Ew!" Spaulding threw the thing down and stomped it into the dirt, rubbing at his head where it had been.

"By attaching a fragment of himself to a victim, the sorcerer is able to observe anyone he chooses. It's magical surveillance." Mr. Radzinsky checked Lucy and Marietta and assured them they were clean. He frowned at Spaulding. "Where did you run into someone powerful enough to do that kind of magic? I question the company you're keeping, I really do."

Spaulding scratched his head again—his skin still felt crawly at the thought of the bug being stuck to him since who-knew-when. "I think it's the same person who's been caus-ing the disturbance in the world of the dead you mentioned before. I guess they can do more than just necromancy."

Mr. Radzinsky crouched down to look at the bug more closely. "Perhaps you'd better get away from this device before we discuss things any further. I think—"

Before he could finish, the bug began to glow faintly red. There was a crackle like electricity, and a spark of reddish light jumped from the bug to the ghost. Mr. Radzinsky looked down at his chest, patting anxiously at himself where the spark had disappeared. "Oh, dear," he said.

"What was that?" Lucy whispered.

Mr. Radzinsky was trembling faintly. The trembling rapidly became twitching. His head began to wrench from side to side. Then a strange, hollow voice spoke. It came from Mr. Radzinsky, but it wasn't his usual voice at all.

"Return . . ." the voice hissed, "*Return what you have stolen . . .*"

Everyone backed away from the ghost except Spaulding. He steeled his nerves and took a step forward. "Mr. Radzinsky?" he whispered, cautiously stretching a hand toward him.

Mr. Radzinsky shuddered, his body curled up in midair as if he was racked with pain. Then he suddenly straightened up, like he'd thrown something heavy off his shoulders.

"Not . . . not me," he gasped in his normal voice. "Sorry— trying to fight it—" He broke off with a choking sound.

"The red mercury!" Lucy said, clutching Spaulding's arm. "You said it gives control over the dead!"

Spaulding nodded. "You're right—I guess that means power over ghosts, too."

Mr. Radzinsky hunched over again, his face hidden in his hands. Slowly, he lifted his head to look at them—but he did it by twisting his head around backward and upside-down. His eyes were glowing a deep, pulsating red.

"*Return what you stole, little boy,*" he said in a nasty sing-song, "*or Auntie and Daddy are going to die.*"

Then he winked out, like a match dropped in water.

Lucy burst out crying again. Spaulding felt like he was frozen in place, staring at the empty air where Mr. Radzinsky had been.

A vise-like hand landed on his shoulder. He flinched and whirled around, half-expecting to see a revenant or the possessed version of Mr. R staring back at him, but it was worse: a very angry-looking Marietta.

"What," she said through her teeth, "*exactly* have you done?"

Chapter Sixteen

Note to Self: Kenny Really
Needs His Beauty Sleep

No one was speaking to Spaulding. Lucy was furious that he had hidden the book from her. Marietta was furious about both the book *and* the fact that he'd taken Lucy into the factory.

"This isn't fair," he grumbled for the hundredth time as they pedaled toward Kenny's house.

Marietta shot him a glare over her shoulder but didn't reply.

"How was I supposed to know this would happen?" Spaulding demanded.

Lucy heaved a sigh. "*Everybody* knows if you find something magic and you take it with you, you'll be sorry. That's like, Rule Number One of snooping around in sorcerer's lairs or ancient tombs or *anywhere*."

"Well, I was going to take it back! Sometime. I just wanted to look at it a little first."

Marietta screeched to a gravel-spitting stop in Kenny's driveway. "The bottom line is," she said, "this whole mess is your fault. But at least now we know what we have to do to fix it. Let's just make sure Kenny's okay, and then we'll go turn over the book."

Kenny's house was dark and quiet. Whether this was a good sign or a bad one was hard to know. However, after a few minutes of throwing pebbles, Kenny's window flew open. There was a terrible groan, and a puffy, squinting face peered out.

GROAAANNNN

Not a revenant, despite terrifying appearance.

HEY! I WAS SLEEPY OK!

STOP WRITING JUNK IN HERE ABOUT ME DUDE

"This'd better be good," Kenny yawned, rubbing his eyes. "I—whoa, what happened? You guys look terrible."

Marietta answered before Spaulding had a chance. "Spaulding has gotten us into an even worse mess than we were in before. Our dad and Spaulding's aunt have been kidnapped because Spaulding stole something from the factory. You'd better go check on your family and make sure they didn't get taken, too."

Kenny's face went white, but he pulled himself together quickly. He disappeared from the window without another word. After a moment or two, the front door opened, and he tiptoed out. "They're sleeping. Everything's locked up tight."

Spaulding nodded. "That makes sense. They targeted us because they were watching me through the bug, and Lucy was with me when I took the book. But they've never seen Kenny, so they don't know he's involved."

Marietta gave a loud sigh. "Just further confirmation that this is your fault. If you hadn't taken my sister into the factory with you—"

"For the millionth time, I'm sorry!"

"He couldn't stop me from going!" Lucy planted her fists on her hips and tried to look tough.

Marietta opened her mouth to yell at both of them, but Kenny interrupted. "You guys, drop it! Let's just get this stupid book from Spaulding's house and hand it over. If we hurry, we can be done in time to catch some more Zs before school.

Being out all night might be okay for *some* people, but I have a big game tomorrow."

Spaulding held up his backpack. "Good news—I have the book with me."

Marietta squinted at him. "You don't *look* like you think it's good news. You look worried. You're not going to argue about handing it over, are you?"

"It's not that. It's just . . . I'm afraid it might not be so simple. Once we turn over the book, why would they let us go? I think we need an insurance policy before we face them."

"An insurance policy?" Marietta wrapped one of her curls around her finger and tugged it thoughtfully. "You mean, some way to make sure Von Slecht doesn't dare hurt us? Like what?"

"Well, Von Slecht is using *our* families against us. How about we do the same to him?"

Marietta raised an eyebrow. "What do you know about his family? I don't know anything about his personal life."

Spaulding grabbed his notebook and showed her the page with his notes from the visit to the factory.

"That's his wife. Lucy and I saw her when we were at the factory. There's something wrong with her—she was getting treatment from Dr. Darke, and she seemed really loopy, like she was drugged or something. If we can get into their house, I don't think it would be hard to trick her into coming with us. Then we hold her captive until Von Slecht releases Aunt Gwen and Mr. Bellwood and lets us all go safely."

Kenny scratched his head. "I don't know. Von Slecht's not going to be exactly terrified that a bunch of kids have his wife. He won't believe we'd hurt anybody."

Spaulding grinned. "I've already figured that part out. Von Slecht knows *we* wouldn't hurt Griselda, but we also have an extremely dangerous boa

Griselda Von Slecht

Super fancy, but lacks something in the personality department.

constrictor on our side. If *he* has her, who knows what might happen?"

Marietta folded her arms. "Nice plan, but you forget—Mr. Radzinsky is the only one who can communicate with David Boa, and *he's* turned evil."

Spaulding's face fell. "Oh. I did forget about that."

Then a gloomy voice spoke from somewhere overhead. "Don't be so melodramatic—I'm not *evil*." Mr. Radzinsky floated down to join them, looking extremely annoyed, but not red-eyed and twitchy anymore. "I was momentarily overpowered, that's all."

"Mr. R!" Spaulding exclaimed.

Kenny screamed and leaped backward, tripped over his own feet, and landed on the sidewalk. "Whozat? And why's he see-through?" he wheezed.

Marietta sighed impatiently. "Jeez, Kenny. That's Spaulding's ghost neighbor. We told you about him, remember?"

"No offense, Mr. R.," Spaulding said cautiously, "but maybe you should stay home. We can't take any chances on having you turn on us all of a sudden."

Mr. Radzinsky sniffed and flicked a bit of ghost lint off his bathrobe. "They took me by surprise. Now that I know what to expect, it won't happen again." He folded his arms and looked down his nose at Spaulding. "Anyway, I am afraid I must insist on accompanying you. You're in much more danger than I realized before, and I've found I feel rather *responsible* for you."

Spaulding felt a sudden tightness in this throat. Mr. Radzinsky might be kind of a jerk . . . and dead . . . *and* crazy . . . but sometimes he could surprise you.

"Okay, Mr. R," he said, taking a deep breath and giving the ghost a nod. "If you say you're okay, I trust you. And . . . I'm glad you're coming."

Mr. Radzinsky gave the lapels of his bathrobe a tug. "I should think you would be! I'll be a great help, obviously."

Spaulding just grinned. Of course Mr. R would try to play it cool—but Spaulding saw a bright pink tinge creep into the green glow of the ghost's sunken cheeks.

Chapter Seventeen

Note to Self: Must Stop Bearding Lions in Dens

Von Slecht Manor stood at the edge of town behind a tall, wrought-iron gate. In the old days when the mining business was booming, the family had been one of the richest in the county, possibly even the whole state, and the manor was still the biggest and fanciest house in Thedgeroot. Not too far away, just on the other side of a wooded hill, the factory smokestacks were faintly visible against the black sky.

Kenny and Lucy huddled down in the shrubbery by the gate while Spaulding and Marietta set off toward the house. Mr. Radzinsky had gone to track down David Boa.

Spaulding and Marietta stayed in the shadow of the tall evergreen hedge bordering the graveled drive. The vast bulk of the mansion glimmered faintly in the moonlight, its windows dark except for one light burning in a downstairs window.

Typical overdone Evil Lair style...
villains really do not seem to know when enough is enough.

"If we're lucky, that means he's still up working and Grisel-da's alone," Spaulding said. "Come on, let's look for a way in."

Spaulding took a step forward, but Marietta grabbed his sleeve. "Wait."

He waited.

She scowled at the ground, gnawing her bottom lip. Finally she burst out, "I'm sorry. You know, about before."

Spaulding stared at her. Then he shrugged. "Fine. Sure." He moved to walk away.

Marietta jumped in front of him, glaring. "Hang on! That's it? That's how you accept my apology?"

He folded his arms and glared back. "I guess I don't accept it, actually. Maybe 'sorry' doesn't really cut it." He skirted around her and stalked off again.

"Hey! That's not fair!" she whisper-yelled behind him. "When people apologize, you accept. That's how it works!"

"Drop it, Marietta," he hissed over his shoulder. "Is now really the best time for this? We're kind of in the middle of something, if you haven't noticed."

She paused. Then she ducked her head. "You're right. So you're willing to let it go for now?"

"Sure."

"Okay." She took a deep breath and gave a little nod. "Cool."

They started walking again, Marietta hurrying ahead.

"Yep. Cool," Spaulding muttered at her back. "I'm willing to just forget about you totally betraying me. No problem."

Marietta whirled around and stabbed a finger at him. "I knew it! I *knew* you were still mad." She stomped back and put her hands on her hips. "Look, I know it was awful that I told Katrina. And I'm really, really sorry. But how can I fix it now? I can't untell her."

He sighed. "I know. There's nothing you can do now." After a moment, he took a deep breath and gave her a small smile. "I guess it'll be good enough to know you're sorry."

She nodded, an uneasy wrinkle still creasing her forehead as she turned away.

At the side of the house, a small servants' entrance was half-hidden in a mass of ivy. Spaulding jiggled the door handle, but it didn't budge.

"Duh, Spaulding, *obviously* the villain keeps his house locked." Marietta elbowed him aside and pointed out a keypad beside the door, smiling rather smugly. "Fortunately, I took the liberty of reading my dad's security files. Mr. Von Slecht's password for absolutely everything is *Griselda*. Dad's told him it's a huge security risk, but he won't listen, so I guess this serves him right."

She punched the code into the keypad. A light above the doorknob flashed green, and the lock clicked softly. She opened the door, and they stepped into Von Slecht Manor.

Spaulding tried to pull the door shut behind him, but something blocked it.

There was an irritated *sss!* from floor-level. He looked down to see David's blunt snout pinched in the door. The snake shoved his way in, Mr. Radzinsky floating close behind.

"Greetings, all!" the ghost trilled, drifting carelessly through Spaulding's body. "We meet again, ho ho!"

Spaulding rubbed at the goose bumps on his arms, scowling at the ghost's back. Mr. R. seemed practically invigorated. It was like he thought they were all out on a nice picnic instead of a desperate mission to save kidnapping victims. Still, he made a good sidekick—he didn't have to worry about getting caught. He led the way, scouting ahead to make sure there was no one around.

Spaulding and Marietta followed through the kitchen and down a long hallway to a marble-floored foyer. Several closed doors led off the foyer, and a sliver of light glowed around one.

Mr. Radzinsky thrust his head through the door of the lighted room. He pulled back quickly and hissed to Spaulding and Marietta, "Von Slecht's in there working. He's alone."

The ghost led the way up the grand staircase. Upstairs, he floated down the hall, sticking his head through each door in turn. At the last one on the right, he pulled his head back and waved them over.

"She's sleeping," he whispered.

As quietly as he could, Spaulding opened the door.

The master bedroom was, at first glance, a perfectly normal room. It kind of looked like a crazy French king should live in it, but still, it was basically normal.

Just your regular fancy-person room!

fancy painting

fancy patterns on every possible surface

sculpture so fancy it's just a blob

fancy bed — but this is where it gets weird...

Some kind of anti-aging treatment?
Rich people are SO weird.

Spaulding took a cautious step closer. Griselda's eyes were open, but she didn't move.

Marietta covered her mouth, horrified. "She's dead!"

Griselda sat up.

Spaulding sighed. "But, as usual, not *dead*-dead. Nobody around here ever is."

He picked up an unlabeled pill bottle from the bedside table. He shook out a pill and examined it. It left a familiar red powder on his fingertips.

Marietta put her hands on her hips. "You know, now

Mr. Von Slecht *is* starting to bug me. What kind of person would marry somebody undead?" She eyed Griselda, who stared back vacantly, her full red lips parted slightly. "She's so . . . boring."

"Isn't she lovely, though?" Mr. Radzinsky exclaimed.

Marietta scowled at him.

"Maybe he loved her before she died, and he couldn't let her go." Spaulding nerved himself up for a second before reaching out to touch the dead woman's arm. To his relief, it felt pretty much like a normal arm, except very cold and firm. "At least we won't have any trouble getting her to cooperate. Come along now, ma'am."

Griselda rose from her freezer-bed and stood beside him awaiting instruction. Marietta pursed her lips, disgusted.

"Mr. R., will you make sure it's safe to go back out?" Spaulding asked.

The ghost nodded and disappeared, returning a few seconds later to report that Von Slecht was still in his study. They hurried quietly into the hall. There was no worry about Griselda making any noise; she drifted along as silent as a dandelion seed.

Downstairs, Marietta raced ahead to the front door, with Spaulding only a few steps behind. This was amazing—their plan was going perfectly! Von Slecht would be stunned when he realized they weren't just a bunch of dumb kids he could push around.

Spaulding gave Griselda's hand a tug, hurrying her out onto the porch—

And an ear-splitting siren shattered the quiet night.

Spaulding and Marietta clapped their hands over their ears and stared at each other in horror. Somehow, Griselda had set off an alarm.

We're dead, Marietta mouthed to Spaulding, the words inaudible under the clamor.

Spaulding couldn't move. It was over. Von Slecht would be out of his study in a heartbeat, and he'd kill Aunt Gwen, and—

Mr. Radzinsky leaned in front of him and looked into his eyes. "You don't have time to be afraid," he said quietly. "*Run!*"

Across the foyer, Von Slecht burst out of his study and took in the scene with a look of dawning fury. He pointed at Spaulding, his finger trembling with rage. "Unhand my wife."

At last, Spaulding pulled himself together. He ran for it, dragging Griselda along behind. She couldn't move quickly, but Marietta grabbed her other hand, and between the two of them, they urged her into a speedier shamble.

Von Slecht's footfalls pounded after them, but he didn't seem to be used to running. Even at Griselda's pace, they were leaving him behind.

"Go! Go!" Mr. Radzinsky floated in front of them, looking back. "You're getting away! He's turned aside—he's gone into—into—oh, dear."

"What?" Spaulding risked a look back. "Where's he gone?"

There was no sign of Von Slecht. Then a blinding light stabbed through the dark, lighting up an enormous swath of the driveway. An engine roared to life. Headlights jerked into motion.

"We can't outrun him if he's in a car!" Marietta cried.

Up ahead, Kenny and Lucy had gotten the bikes out of the bushes and were waiting at the end of the driveway. "What's going on? What's that noise?" Kenny yelled as they ran up.

"There was an alarm rigged to sound if Griselda left the house," Spaulding panted. "He's behind us in his car."

"Let's cut through the fields, then!" Lucy said. She was already on her bike, holding the handlebars of Spaulding's with her free hand. "He can't drive out there. It's way too marshy for a truck, but I know a path we can take the bikes on."

"But how do we take Griselda on our bikes?" Marietta asked.

Spaulding looked back. The headlights were getting closer, fast. "Forget the bikes—he'll have to take the road or else follow on foot, so speed shouldn't matter as much."

They dropped the bikes and dove off the side of the road into the tall grass.

Seconds later, Von Slecht came roaring down the driveway. The headlights fell on the abandoned bikes in the road. The vehicle screeched to a halt. The roar of the engine fell to a growl.

Spaulding peered through the weeds.

A truck idled in the road. Its tires were as tall as a regular car. A row of high-powered lights topped the cab. The windows were tinted pure black, so the driver was invisible. But Spaulding knew Von Slecht was in there, his watery eyes scanning the darkness for the slightest movement.

Spaulding held his breath, hoping he wouldn't somehow draw Von Slecht's gaze by staring so hard.

Finally, in a spray of gravel, the truck roared away. There was an awful crunching and popping sound like snapping bones as it went—Von Slecht had run over the bikes.

Kenny jumped to his feet. "Let's go!"

They started out across the field.

Thrashing through the long grass was worse than Spaulding had expected. The thick, wet blades tangled around their legs. They kept falling over hidden rocks and stepping into holes. Spaulding gritted his teeth, expecting to snap an ankle any second. Griselda wasn't slowing them down anymore—no one could move fast.

The truck's engine had been getting fainter, but suddenly it gave a throaty roar.

Spaulding looked back and almost let out a sob. They'd hardly covered any ground at all. And Von Slecht must have suspected he was going the wrong way, because the truck had turned around.

The headlights swept across the field. Four kids, one dead woman, and one ghost were pinned in light as bright as day. The truck lunged forward—straight toward them.

"He's driving right across the field!" Spaulding tried to move faster. He yanked on Griselda's cold hand.

Marietta just stood, staring at the giant vehicle. "We can't outrun him."

Spaulding tried to think, but he felt stunned by the blinding lights. Even Mr. Radzinsky was silent.

Only Kenny kept running. "Come on, come on! You can't give—*aaaagh!*"

He had vanished mid-sentence.

"What on earth—" Spaulding edged toward where Kenny had disappeared. "Kenny?"

"Oww." Kenny's voice sounded nearby but muffled. "Why didn't we bring a flashlight?" he groaned.

Spaulding dug into his backpack. "I *always* bring a flashlight."

"I fell into some kind of pit," Kenny called.

Marietta gasped. "A mine shaft! They're all over the place out here."

Spaulding swept his flashlight beam around until he spotted a black pit hidden in the grass a few yards away. He edged up to the brink and peered down. Kenny's pale face gazed up at him from perhaps fifteen feet below.

"You gotta lower a rope or something," Kenny said.

Spaulding shook his head. "Nope," he said as Von Slecht's truck roared again. "Get out of the way—we're coming down there!"

Chapter Eighteen

Note to Self: Get Over Fear of Enclosed, Dark Spaces Because Apparently Destined to Spend a Lot of Time in Them

Getting into the pit was easy enough. One side of the hole was a slope of loose dirt and gravel where the roof of the mine had caved in, and they half-walked, half-slid down. Ahead of them, the tunnel was intact. It slanted downward, deeper into the earth.

Still, the darkness was practically inviting compared to the roaring of the truck, which was so loud Spaulding figured Von Slecht must be almost overhead now. They hurried a few yards down the tunnel until the sound was muffled.

"Can't we just hide here until he leaves?" Lucy whispered.

Spaulding shook his head. "It won't take him long to figure out where we went. Our only chance is to keep going."

"But we'll get lost," Kenny moaned. "This could go on for miles and miles and connect to other tunnels, and there could be dead guys down here and stuff."

Hooray! Was hoping it was time for another terrifying descent into the bowels of the earth.

Marietta snapped her fingers. "My map!" She dug in her pocket and pulled out a paper folded into a small, dirty square. She'd clearly been carrying it for a while. "It's not completely accurate, but it ought to give us some idea of where we are."

She unfolded it and they all leaned in to see. Marietta traced her finger along a line that went past the field where Von Slecht's house now stood. "That looks like about the area we're in—somewhere in this small tunnel off the main shaft. You're lucky you fell into this little tunnel, Kenny. The main shaft probably goes down hundreds of feet." She made a long, whistling, falling sound, ending in a juicy *splat*.

Kenny glared. "Thank you for that, Marietta. That's very nice to think about right now."

"I'm only trying to look at the bright side!" she protested, widening her eyes. "Anyway, let's keep going." She tapped the map again. "We need to find another tunnel up to the surface. Watch where you step, though. Sometimes they'd dig shafts straight down to look for new veins, and then they'd put planks over the top to walk on. Only by now, the planks will be too rotten to hold weight. So if your footsteps sound hollow—"

"I'd never have believed it, Marietta," Kenny interrupted, smirking. "Turns out you're a bigger nerd than Spaulding. You're, like, a *mining nerd*. I didn't even know there was such a thing."

"I am not!" she huffed. "It's not nerdy to know about cool stuff like exploring mines! I shouldn't even warn you about the ant traps. That'd serve you right."

Kenny froze midstep. "What the heck are ant traps?" he demanded.

"That's when a vertical shaft collapses into a funnel. It just looks like a little sunken place, but if you put weight on it, it'll give way, and—" She gave another cheery *splat*.

"Okay, that is it." Kenny folded his arms. "I'm not going down a tunnel full of death traps just hoping some antique map keeps me alive and unlost. No way."

"Now, now," Mr. Radzinsky said kindly. "You forget, I can pop up to the surface anytime and see where we are. I won't let you get lost."

Kenny muttered something about Mr. Radzinsky not being able to prevent them from falling into hidden deadly pits of doom, but there wasn't any choice except to go on.

Slowly, they went in deeper. The floor was lumpy and uneven; the air frigid and damp. Mr. Radzinsky's glow cast odd, lurching shadows, and Spaulding kept thinking he saw things moving out of the corner of his eye. Marietta stopped frequently to check the map, but it didn't seem to be particularly accurate, and they couldn't be sure how far they'd gone.

Eventually, they came to a fork in the tunnel. Everyone stopped and looked at Marietta.

She dragged in a deep breath. "Okay, I'm pretty sure we want to go right. It looks like it goes up to the surface. Left just seems to go deeper into the mine."

Mr. Radzinsky floated down the left-hand tunnel until he disappeared around a corner. He reappeared quickly. "Hopefully you're right," he said brightly. "That way is caved in."

They turned right. The new tunnel sloped up quickly, and a breeze promised fresh air close ahead. After a quick scramble over some loose dirt and rocks that were heaped at the tunnel mouth, they found themselves back on the surface.

Spaulding gasped in a mouthful of air. Pushing past the others, he staggered forward without a thought except putting distance between himself and the mine. But he'd only gone a step when something slammed into him from behind and knocked him to the ground.

He rolled over, dazed, as Marietta scrambled to her feet. "Excuse you, Marietta!" he puffed.

"Well, if you'd watch where you're going, I wouldn't have had to do that!"

She gestured to a harmless-looking sunken spot in the ground a few feet away. "That," she said, "is an ant trap."

Spaulding stared at the small, dark hole at the center of the sunken area. "You mean—if I'd stepped onto the edge . . ."

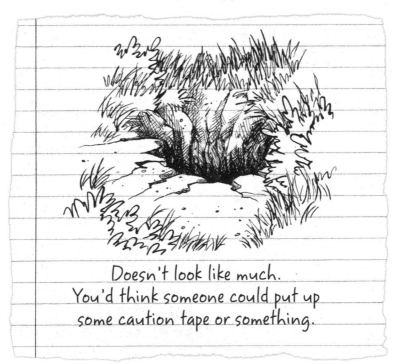

Doesn't look like much.
You'd think someone could put up
some caution tape or something.

She scooted a half-step closer and peered down. "There's no way to tell how deep it is for sure, but the map shows a two-hundred-foot air shaft near here."

Spaulding swallowed, staring at the pit. "Oh. Well. I guess saving my life makes up for, you know, the other thing."

Marietta scowled at the ant trap as if it had personally offended her. She muttered something that Spaulding couldn't quite catch, but it sounded like "No, it doesn't."

The moment was just starting to feel extremely awkward when Kenny interrupted. Unfortunately, he interrupted with a string of loud kissy noises, making it several hundred million times more awkward.

Luckily, Lucy interrupted him before Marietta could locate a murder weapon. "Have you guys noticed where we are?" she asked.

For the first time, Spaulding took a real look around. They were back in the woods. Just ahead, a weedy bank sloped down to a familiar dark shape—Blackhope Pond.

At that moment, an engine roared to life somewhere very close by. A pair of blinding lights stabbed through the trees, and branches snapped and splintered as Von Slecht's truck plunged straight toward them.

Spaulding's heart jumped into his throat.

"He was waiting for us!" Marietta gasped. "He must have known the mine tunnel ended up here."

"We're going to have to make our stand now," Spaulding

said. He hoped he sounded calm and determined instead of pants-wettingly terrified. "Mr. Radzinsky, can you tell David to hold Griselda and look like he'll eat her if we give the word?"

"Of course," Mr. Radzinsky said. He knelt in front of the snake, who reared up his head to gaze into the ghost's eyes.

Spaulding left them to their silent communication and turned to the others. "You guys make a circle around Griselda and block Von Slecht if he tries to get to her."

On the far side of the pond, the truck jerked to a stop. Von Slecht cut the engine. The only sound was the ticking of cooling metal.

Spaulding wiped his hands on his pajama bottoms.

At last, the driver's side door opened, and Von Slecht stepped out. He gave them all a long, unblinking stare.

"Release my wife and hand over the book immediately," he said, his voice soft, "and I won't kill you."

Spaulding squared his shoulders. "Only after you let my aunt and Mr. Bellwood go. Otherwise . . ." He stepped aside, revealing David Boa wrapped around Griselda's body. The snake obligingly opened his jaws wide behind her head and hissed. ". . . I'm afraid she's dinner."

"You think you can intimidate me?" Von Slecht snorted. "With a dumb animal that I happen to know has never eaten a human being in his life? Pathetic." He snapped his fingers. "Griselda, come here."

Griselda attempted to stand up, struggling against the boa constrictor's weight.

"I can't believe I ever looked up to you," Marietta snapped at Von Slecht. She put a hand on Griselda's shoulder and pushed her back down. "I mean, you're married to a *corpse*! What is *wrong* with you?"

"Quite a lovely corpse, though," Mr. Radzinsky murmured to no one in particular.

A red flush crept up Von Slecht's face. "You could never understand how deeply I love her. Even death couldn't change that."

Spaulding had a flash of understanding. "Griselda was the first," he said suddenly.

Von Slecht paused, one hand stretched toward his wife.

"All the workers," Spaulding continued, "the free labor with no vacation days and no rights—that idea came later. You learned to raise the dead just to bring her back, didn't you?"

Von Slecht laughed uneasily, his eyes darting. "Is this the part where I explain my evil plot? No, thanks."

Spaulding shrugged. "It doesn't matter—I already get it. Your whole business is making red mercury just to keep some dead lady preserved. It's pointless."

"You know about the red mercury?" Von Slecht demanded. He pulled a handkerchief from his pocket and dabbed at a bead of sweat on his brow. "Well, well. Darke said I underestimated you. And yet, clever as you may be, you still don't understand the greatness of what I've done." He took a step closer, his voice dropping to a hoarse whisper. "Yes, I sank my fortune into bringing my wife back—and I achieved it. Do you understand? I have *undone death*."

Marietta scrunched up her nose. "Yeah. Great work. Is that how you put your family's factory out of business?"

Von Slecht sputtered, balling his handkerchief in his fist. "What—it—it's *not* out of business! My plan is simply more long-term than you can wrap your mind around. You're as short-sighted as my mother."

"What, the tunnels?" Spaulding asked. He rolled his eyes. "Sure, I'll bet there's *tons* of money to make in the big-holes-in-the-ground industry."

"It's not about money, you fool!" Von Slecht's voice shot up an octave. "It's about *power*. Why would I stick to simply running a factory when I have an unlimited workforce at my disposal? And a system of mines already in existence, just waiting to be expanded? Have you any idea how far those tunnels go?"

"No," Spaulding said.

"No." A smile crept over Von Slecht's face, revealing the grayish teeth in his wide jaw. "You don't. And neither does the government, or the army, or the National Guard. With my tunnels, I can move my army of deathless soldiers into position to overthrow the government before they even know what's happening. I'll be unstoppable, and together Griselda and I will rule *forever!*"

"He's raising an army?" Marietta gave Spaulding a kick to the sneaker. "I told you we should have gone to the police!"

Spaulding's hands were shaking. She was right. Of course she was right. This was completely out of control. He'd made a huge mistake by not going straight to the police. But maybe there was still a way around that error.

"I know you did, Marietta." He folded his arms and attempted to give Von Slecht a tough-guy stare. "And guess what? I took your advice. I went to the cops, and I told them everything."

Von Slecht burst out laughing. Not quite the reaction Spaulding had been hoping for.

"The police?" Von Slecht giggled. "Oh good heavens, not the police! Whatever shall I do now?" He laughed harder and harder.

Spaulding stood up as straight as he could. "If we go missing after what I told them, you're going to be their number one suspect."

Von Slecht uncrumpled his handkerchief and dabbed at his eyes, still chuckling. "Oh, dear. Perhaps you aren't so smart after all. Surely you can't have believed you were the only ones in the whole town aware of all this? You never once thought it a little odd that *you*'d ferreted all this out, but the *police* had no idea?"

"The newspaper said the police didn't know what was going on with the grave robberies," Spaulding protested.

"Ah—that little article. I'm afraid that was the work of a certain newly hired editor who didn't have all the facts. She also didn't realize that investigative journalism isn't really welcome here in Thedgeroot. Of course, she moved on to a new career shortly after that." Von Slecht folded his handkerchief back into a tight square and tucked it into his pocket once more. "It turns out she's much better suited to factory work."

Spaulding's stomach gave a sickening flip. Mr. Radzinsky, this newspaper editor . . . how many times had Von Slecht gotten away with murder? And if he'd done it before, there was nothing to stop him from killing them, too. The only possible hold they had over him sat a few feet behind Spaulding, wrapped in boa constrictor.

"You might not be worried about the police," Spaulding said, "but if you don't let our families go, we won't give you back your wife."

The businessman sighed. "This grows tiresome. I don't need you to *give* me my wife." He took a step forward.

"Squeeze, David Boa," Spaulding ordered.

"Don't you dare," Von Slecht growled. He surged toward the snake.

Instantly, Kenny lunged forward too and grabbed Von Slecht from behind. But the businessman broke free easily. Without even looking, he slammed Kenny aside with a backhanded blow.

Kenny landed heavily on his side a few feet away, groaning.

"Oof," he wheezed, clutching his stomach. "He's really strong, guys. I think he's using magic or something."

Von Slecht snorted. "Of course I'm using magic! You little fools have no idea what I'm capable of." Before anyone could react, he shoved Marietta and Spaulding aside and reached for Griselda. "Come, my darling."

He pulled her to her feet, grabbed David around the neck, and flung him away—or rather, he tried to fling him away. But the snake was too fast. In a blur, David whipped his tail up and wrapped it around Von Slecht's arm. Von Slecht lost his hold on Griselda, who stumbled a few steps.

David Boa lashed himself around Von Slecht's torso, pinning his left arm against his side. But Von Slecht's right arm was free. He seized the boa in an iron grip, his hand squeezing just behind David's jaws.

"What can we do?" Marietta demanded.

"I don't know!" Spaulding looked around helplessly—there was nothing to hit Von Slecht with, and no way to do it without hitting David too.

Spaulding's eyes fell on Griselda. She'd managed to stay on her feet and keep walking. She seemed unaware of the fight—unaware of everything, really. The moon had just cleared the treetops, and she was staring up into its cold light. Spaulding wondered afterward if she was staggering toward that. Maybe she was moving mindlessly. Or maybe some remaining shred of her mind knew this was her chance to escape.

Whatever the reason, she was headed straight toward the ant trap.

"Watch out!" he cried as she took the final step that put her weight on the loose earth.

With a soft *shushhh*, the slope of loose earth shifted and Griselda's feet slid out from under her. She landed on her back, her falling weight speeding the landslide.

Spaulding took a step toward her, but Marietta caught his wrist. "You'd just fall too," she said quietly.

Von Slecht turned his head in time to see Griselda vanish into the hole. He gave a strangled, wordless cry. Before anyone else could move, he threw himself into the pit after her.

He screamed as he fell. It went on and on, until finally it cut off abruptly. A thick, awful silence fell. Von Slecht was gone at last.

But so was David Boa.

Chapter Nineteen

Note to Self: Never Make Mr. Radzinsky Angry

The woods and the pond were quiet. The only sound came from the edge of the pit where Mr. Radzinsky crouched, quietly sobbing as he stared down into the darkness.

Spaulding and Marietta looked at each other. She gave her chin a little jerk away from the ghost. Spaulding nodded, and the four walked out of his earshot.

"So that's it, then," Kenny said quietly. "It's over. Von Slecht couldn't have survived a fall like that. That *scream*." He shivered.

"All we have to do now is find Dad and your aunt," Lucy said.

Marietta sighed. "Yeah,

but what about him?" She nodded toward Mr. Radzinsky. "He's not going to want to leave yet, and he can't stay here alone."

"I'll keep an eye on him," Spaulding said. "I'm his friend. You guys can find Aunt Gwen and your dad without me. I'm sure they're at the factory. Mr. R. already looked in most of the rooms at the manor."

"I'll stay with you, Spaulding," Lucy offered. "You shouldn't be alone either."

He smiled. "Thanks, Lucy."

Spaulding showed Marietta the drain tunnel that led to the factory and loaned her his flashlight, and she and Kenny set off. Spaulding and Lucy went to sit beside Mr. Radzinsky.

The ghost didn't look up, but he heaved a deep sigh as they approached. "I know I have to go down there and look, but I can't seem to make myself do it just yet," he said.

Lucy gasped. "Oh, no, don't do that!"

Spaulding nodded. "She's right, Mr. R. You shouldn't do that to yourself. It'll only make you feel worse."

"But he's alone down there," the ghost said, his voice cracking on the word *alone*.

"Don't think of it like that," Lucy said, sniffling. "He's not *really* down there. He's gone. Or if he's not gone—if he's like you—then he isn't stuck down there."

Spaulding cleared his aching throat. "He was a great snake, Mr. Radzinsky."

Mr. Radzinsky smiled weakly.

"Yeah," Lucy agreed. "If it wasn't for him, we wouldn't have won."

"Now, on *that* point," said a voice close behind them, "I am forced to correct you."

Slowly, with a feeling like ice trickling down his neck, Spaulding turned. Standing not ten feet away, immaculate as ever in a shiny black suit, was Dr. Darke.

She strolled toward them, perfectly steady on the uneven ground despite her very pointy heels. Behind her, at least a hundred revenants appeared from the woods, moving with unusual speed and coordination.

"You see," she said, "you haven't won at all."

Oops. Kinda forgot about her...

"I would have come sooner," the doctor continued, "but I didn't think poor, stupid Werner would need my help to deal with a bunch of children. It seems I overestimated him once again."

Spaulding jumped to his feet and backed away, pulling Lucy along with him. Mr. Radzinsky positioned himself in front of them, but Spaulding could see he was still shaken and weak. The glow he cast wavered fitfully, like a candle about to go out.

Lucy's fingers dug painfully into Spaulding's arm. "But Von Slecht is gone! The undead were his magic, they should be gone, too."

Dr. Darke gave a sharp laugh. "It surprises me you thought I'd let him have any *real* power. I gave him a little spell to work here and there so he'd feel important, but I'm the true necromancer. All he was good for was providing money."

Her voice deepened and echoed oddly. For a moment, Spaulding thought he saw a yellow light glint at the back of her eyes. He had a peculiar sense of something *larger* in her body with her.

Mr. Radzinsky drew himself up tall. "Stop right where you are," he snapped. "These children are under my protection."

Dr. Darke's eyes widened. For an instant, Spaulding thought she was afraid. Then she laughed.

"How quaint," she said, and waved a hand.

Mr. Radzinsky blew apart, scattered like dandelion seeds. "Drat," Spaulding heard him mutter faintly as the cloud of glowing green specks dispersed.

Spaulding looked around wildly. There had to be something—a weapon, a way to signal Kenny and Marietta to come back . . .

The doctor smiled. "No one will hear you screaming for help—not that I'll give you a chance to." The revenants streamed past her in a gibbering horde. "I'm not soft-hearted about children like poor old Werner was."

"This isn't fair!" Lucy stomped her foot. "We had a plan, and it worked. We won!"

"Would you just run?" Spaulding hauled her to her feet and took off toward Von Slecht's truck, the howling mob of undead just behind them. He yanked open the rear door and vaulted inside, climbing into the front seat to give Lucy room to get in.

But Daphne was slowing Lucy down. She was still several steps behind. As she reached for the back seat to haul herself up, one of the faster corpses leaped forward. Its bony fingers snagged the euphonium's valves. Lucy stumbled, and the revenant pounced.

"Help!" Lucy screamed just outside Spaulding's door.

The revenant bent over her, its rotten mouth open wide.

Spaulding peered down from his window. The truck was so tall . . . and Lucy was flat on the ground . . . it might work. It was the only idea he had, anyway.

"Keep your head down, Lucy," he muttered. Then he squeezed his eyes shut and wrenched his door open as hard as he could.

There was a sound like an egg cracking. The undead thing staggered backward with a squeal, clutching its head. Spaulding leaned out and grabbed Lucy's hand. She scrambled up into the truck, and he slammed the door and punched the lock button. They were safe for the moment—though it didn't look like that moment would last long.

The revenants swarmed the truck. Fingernails screeched on the doors and windows. The truck began to sway as some of the smarter creatures began trying to overturn it.

Dr. Darke stood a few yards away, laughing her head off, as if she were watching the best show she'd ever seen.

Mr. Radzinsky materialized in the passenger seat. "Well, I tried," he said, slumping down listlessly. "But I couldn't save you any more than I could save my poor David Boa. Look on the bright side, though—in a few minutes, when you're dead, I'll be right here to guide you."

Spaulding sighed. "I know you're upset, Mr. R, but maybe just keep your thoughts to yourself for a while, okay?" He felt the ignition switch, then pawed through the glove box and under the seat. Nothing.

"The keys aren't here," he said.

"They're with Von Slecht at the bottom of the mine." Lucy hugged Daphne tight, sniffling. At that moment, a white light exploded around them. Lucy screamed. Spaulding grabbed the dashboard. For an instant, the truck seemed to have been engulfed in fire. It rocked onto the passenger-side wheels and then fell back down with a crash.

"What was that?" Lucy panted.

"I think she's tired of waiting." Spaulding peered out at the doctor.

She stabbed a finger at the truck, shouting words he couldn't make out. Another ball of white light began to form around her hands.

"Brace yourself," Mr. Radzinsky said.

Dr. Darke snapped her wrists toward the truck. A crackling, bluish-white bolt of energy rushed toward them. Spaulding and Lucy hunched their shoulders and plugged their ears. But when the bolt hit the truck, it simply disappeared. The vehicle didn't even bounce.

"Nothing happened," Lucy said in surprise.

Then the locks popped up.

"Grab the doors," Spaulding yelled, but it was too late. The doors opened of their own accord, and the undead rushed forward.

"Get to the woods! Maybe we can climb the trees or something." Spaulding threw himself straight at the nearest revenant with all his might, shouldering it aside. Hands clutched at him, but his momentum carried him past. The revenants weren't individually very strong or coordinated—but there were so many of them. It would be impossible to keep shoving through them for long without tiring out.

"I don't see how you're improving your situation," Mr. Radzinsky commented as they reached the edge of the woods.

"You're not helping," Spaulding snapped, fighting through

a thicket of blackberry brambles. "Lucy, let go of Daphne before she gets you killed!"

Lucy's arms were clearly tiring—Daphne was nearly dragging on the ground. But Lucy just clutched the instrument tighter to her chest, as if somehow it could protect her.

Spaulding's breath caught in his throat. What if it *could* protect her? It was a long shot—a *huge* long shot, since it depended on his parents being right about something for once—but it was worth a try.

He grabbed Lucy's arm and pointed to a wide, double-trunked oak a few strides ahead. "When we get to that big tree, duck behind it." They couldn't keep running if his idea was going to have a chance of working—Lucy would have to catch her breath.

An instant later, they crouched down on the far side of the broad tree. The noise of the undead thrashing through the brush sounded nearby, but the revenants were too clumsy to move fast through the thick undergrowth.

"Play something," Spaulding ordered.

Lucy gaped at him. "What? Now? Have you gone crazy?"

"Just do it, Lucy!"

"Oh, fine," she sighed. "What would you like to hear? I don't know what's appropriate for ten seconds before being torn apart."

"Funeral music," Mr. Radzinsky suggested.

Lucy rolled her eyes and took a deep breath.

The first notes spilled forth. Spaulding didn't recognize the piece, but it was soft and mournful. And Daphne didn't sound silly and oompa-oompa like he had imagined. She sounded sweet and gentle, like a sad woman singing about something lost forever.

The sounds of the undead crashing through the woods slowed. Cautiously, Spaulding peered around the side of the oak as the melody continued.

A few feet away, a revenant stumbled toward him. But it wasn't moving normally—its knees were flopping in all directions as though its joints no longer connected properly. Then one leg fell apart completely. Its shin, knee, and thigh bones toppled like a crumbling tower of blocks. The revenant stood for an instant, swaying, and then it fell to pieces. With one last, fading wheeze, its body sank in on itself. Nothing was left but a husk of dry skin and disconnected bones.

Everywhere Spaulding looked, other revenants were stumbling and sinking to the ground. As the music swelled to a crescendo, the last stragglers laid themselves down.

"It worked," Spaulding said, eyes wide. "My parents were actually right about something! Music really *does* banish spirits to the Shadow Realms!"

"Only the primitive ones," Mr. Radzinsky sniffed.

Lucy stopped playing. "Can . . . I . . . stop . . . yet?" she wheezed.

Hesitantly, Spaulding crept out from behind the tree and prodded the nearest fallen revenant with his toe. It didn't move. "I think they're really gone," he said.

Mr. Radzinsky nodded. "The spirits animating them departed. They won't easily be called back."

Spaulding ducked behind the tree again. He had a feeling Dr. Darke wasn't far away, and she wouldn't be too happy about losing her minions.

Seconds later, a cold voice spoke, echoing from everywhere at once—the same warped version of Dr. Darke's voice that had spoken through Mr. Radzinsky before. The ghost shuddered at the sound of it. "I won't play hide-and-seek with you," the voice hissed. "Not least because there's nowhere you can hide."

Directly in front of them, the doctor appeared from nowhere. She stretched out a hand. Spaulding felt a soft, feathery touch on his collarbone. Something was twining itself around his neck. But when he felt with his hands, there was nothing there. He looked at Lucy. She was patting at her neck in confusion, too.

The invisible thing crept up the sides of his face. It tightened around his neck. He clawed at his throat harder, trying to find some grip on it, but there was just nothing there . . .

"That is quite enough!" Mr. Radzinsky shouted.

The doctor didn't even turn her head. "Oh, dear," she smirked. "Have you forgotten you're incorporeal? You can't stop me. Nothing you do matters."

Mr. Radzinsky clawed at her face, his own face turning hideous and distorted. But his hands passed right through her.

The nothingness had reached Spaulding's mouth and nose.

It filled them with a downy softness, like a pillow over his face. He pawed at his mouth desperately, but there was no way to fight it.

Blackness began to crawl in from the edges of his vision. He stumbled a step toward Dr. Darke, imagining himself leaping at her and breaking the spell.

She took one slow, leisurely step back and watched him fall to the ground.

His lungs were nearly empty, but he had one last hope. "Mr. R.," he croaked.

The ghost flicked to his side instantly, wringing his hands. "Yes, dear boy?"

"She's . . . the one . . . killed . . . you . . ."

For a moment, the ghost's expression didn't change. Then his face filled with understanding. He looked at the smiling doctor.

"You," he whispered.

Her smile widened. Spaulding had never seen her look so genuinely happy.

"You made me think my best friend killed me."

"That's right," she agreed. "Well, I can't take all the credit—a colleague at the newspaper helped spread the story. After a touch of persuasion, of course."

Mr. Radzinsky's voice grew colder. "You made *everyone* think it. If they'd caught him, they'd have killed him for it."

Spaulding felt a tiny tremor in the ground under his cheek.

Maybe Dr. Darke felt something too, because her smile disappeared. "What difference does it make now?" she snapped. "He's dead anyway."

Mr. Radzinsky's shaking hands clenched into fists. His jaw stretched wide. From his mouth came the most terrifying noise Spaulding had ever heard. It wasn't a roar or a scream—not a human one, anyway. It wasn't even exactly loud. It was more like a *tearing*, like something shredding through the fabric of reality itself.

Dr. Darke clapped her hands over her ears and screamed. The smothering softness melted away from Spaulding's face as the doctor lost her concentration.

The tremors in the ground had grown to earthquake strength. The oak tree groaned and quivered. Spaulding's eyes widened—the giant tree's branches were whipping like a tornado was coming. He grabbed Lucy's arm and they ran blindly away.

He glanced back. Dr. Darke was doubled over, eyes squeezed shut against the pain of the sound. She didn't see what was happening to the oak tree behind her.

But Spaulding saw.

He saw the crack in the double trunk widening like an opening mouth. He saw one half of the huge tree falling, slowly at first but gaining speed rapidly. At the last moment, he shut his eyes. He only heard the splintering crash and the sudden silence as the shrieking abruptly stopped.

Slowly, he opened his eyes, still clutching Lucy's hand.

I can't really say I feel bad about this.

Mr. Radzinsky materialized in front of them, his face back to normal. He gave a small smile. "Well done, my boy," he said quietly. "Well done."

But Spaulding's heart sank as he looked at Mr. Radzinsky. They might have won, but the cost had been steep. "David was amazing, Mr. R.," he said softly.

"He always *was* selfless," Mr. Radzinsky said with a deep sigh. "And he wouldn't want us to sit here forever. I think it's time we go find your families and head home."

Chapter Twenty

Note to Self: Find Nice, Safe Hobby Now That I Am Retired from Paranormal Investigation (Have Heard Good Things about Stamp Collecting)

The sun cut through the clouds on the horizon and lanced through the trees, striping light and shade across the road to Blackhope Pond.

Spaulding didn't know why he and Lucy were out here—a few days ago, he thought he'd never want to set eyes on the pond again. But when he woke on Saturday to a clear morning, the open road beckoned. He dragged Aunt Gwen's creaky old bike out of the garage and set off down the street. Lucy was already outside when he passed the Bellwood residence, and she hopped up on the seat behind him while he pedaled. They headed for the pond without even discussing it.

At the clearing, they got off the bike and walked down to the water's edge. The pond was a light, sparkling blue. Tiny ripples spread across the surface from the breeze. Spaulding sat down next to Lucy and tried to clear his mind. But dark thoughts kept creeping in.

DAVID BOA

HERO, FRIEND, SNAKE

"Are you thinking about David?" Lucy asked.

Spaulding sighed. "Yeah. I have been all week. It's so unfair. He never did anything wrong, and he saved us all from Von Slecht."

"And poor ol' Mr. Radzinsky," Lucy said. "Have you noticed how faded he's looking?"

Spaulding hugged his knees to his chest. A heavy, clammy, nameless feeling settled over him. He'd first felt it that night, soon after they'd defeated Dr. Darke . . .

When he and Lucy and Mr. Radzinsky had arrived at the factory, they'd found Kenny and Marietta still crouched at the end of the drain tunnel, discussing how to get past the revenant guards Dr. Darke had left roaming around outside. The revenants had all suddenly collapsed and stopped moving a while before, but Kenny was sure they were faking. Marietta hadn't been able to get him to budge.

Even after Spaulding explained what had happened to Dr. Darke, everyone had a creeping fear they would encounter Von Slecht and the doctor inside, somehow alive and lying in wait. But the buildings had been empty and silent. They'd found

Aunt Gwen and Mr. Bellwood in the lab, slumped against a wall with their eyes open, not even tied up.

Marietta had run forward and flung herself at her father. "Dad?" She'd shaken his arm. His head had lolled.

"They're in a trance," Mr. Radzinsky said, peering into Mr. Bellwood's glazed eyes. "I'm sure they'll wake up soon."

Aunt Gwendolyn and Mr. Bellwood had followed along like sleepwalkers as everyone hurried out of the lab.

Spaulding came out last. He took one last look around at the blank computer screens and the canisters of red mercury. What would happen to the factory now? And what about the Slecht-Tech corporate office and the regular, alive-type workers there? With their employers gone, he supposed that meant a whole lot of people out of jobs.

That was when Spaulding had first felt that heavy feeling come over him. He felt like he'd woken something or pushed a boulder down a hill. Like he'd set something bigger than he understood in motion.

He'd flicked off the lights and hurried after the others.

The next morning, Aunt Gwen didn't seem to remember that anything out of the ordinary had happened at all. According to Lucy, it was the same with Mr. Bellwood. All week at school, rumors circulated that Slecht-Tech had closed down, but Lucy said her dad was as puzzled as anyone by the disappearance of Mr. Von Slecht and Dr. Darke. Spaulding had a substitute teacher in homeroom who told the class that Mrs. Welliphaunt had gone to stay with family overseas indefinitely.

Of the dead bodies someone must have found littering the woods, there was no discussion at all. Not among the kids at school and not in the paper.

Marietta had also decided to clam up. She wouldn't talk to either Spaulding or Kenny, and Lucy said she was just as quiet at home. Spaulding wondered if she'd withdrawn from them all because she felt bad that their investigation had nearly gotten her dad hurt. That was how he felt with Aunt Gwen. Every time he saw her, he felt a fresh stab of guilt.

And the thought that it had all happened because he was trying to impress his parents so he could leave Aunt Gwen and live with them was worst of all. Maybe she wasn't the most involved guardian, or overprotective and concerned like Mr. Bellwood was, but it would break her heart if Spaulding left . . . he was pretty sure, anyway.

"Spaulding, look," Lucy said suddenly, making him jump.

Across the pond, Mr. Radzinsky had just materialized from thin air, drifting across the water. "Mr. R.?" Spaulding called. "What are you doing out here?"

The ghost glanced over. "Oh, hello, children. I didn't notice you over there." He floated toward them, the breeze across the pond propelling him. "It's good you're here—I wanted to tell you I was leaving."

"Leaving?" Spaulding demanded. "What do you mean?

You can't just *go*. Aren't you stuck here? Don't ghosts have unfinished business or something?"

"I'm going after David," Mr. Radzinsky said. "He *is* my unfinished business. I go where he goes."

"You mean, you're going to . . ." Spaulding hesitated, trying to think how to put it politely. The only thing that came to mind was a Serena phrase. ". . . cross the veil?"

The ghost snorted. "Cross the veil! Where *do* you get these ideas? I meant I'm going down the mine shaft, obviously. I already looked for him the night he fell—I came back after I saw you home. But he wasn't down there. Neither of them were."

"They got out?" Lucy whipped her head around, panicked. "Von Slecht is still around?"

Mr. Radzinsky shook his head. "No, no. I mean, they weren't there because the bottom of the shaft wasn't there. It didn't end."

Spaulding wrinkled his forehead. "How can it not end? They had to stop digging eventually."

Mr. Radzinsky shrugged. "I don't know. It was like no mine I've ever seen or heard of. No straight lines, no tracks for mine carts, no signs of ore being extracted. Just tunnels, looping and twisting endlessly, with no pattern or reason I could find. I finally gave up." He twisted his hands, glancing at the mouth of the pit from the corner of his eye. "I haven't been frightened of anything since I died, but down there . . . I was afraid. Still, I have to try again."

"But—but—" Spaulding tried to think of a way to convince him not to go even though he knew the ghost would never change his mind. Not when David needed his help. "But you're my friend too." He stared at the ground, blinking hard.

Mr. Radzinsky looked stunned. "Really? I thought you just needed me for my expertise."

Spaulding sniffed and hunched his shoulders so Lucy wouldn't see as he scrubbed at his eyes. "Well, your expertise is one of the reasons I like you. We're both smart."

The ghost put a clammy hand on—or more like in—Spaulding's shoulder. "Thank you, Spaulding. No one's been so kind to me in a long time. But I'll come back once I find David. In the meantime you'll have your other friends."

Spaulding couldn't hold back anymore. "I don't have other friends, Mr. R.," he burst out. "They were just using me for my expertise. Now that the mystery's over, I'll just be the freak nobody wants to be seen with again."

"Spaulding!" Lucy gave him a tremendous wallop to the arm. "What a dumb thing to say! I wasn't using you for your expert tea. I don't even know what that means."

Spaulding sniffled. "It means you only wanted to be around me because I knew about all the weird stuff that was going on."

Mr. Radzinsky chuckled. "Listen, my boy: If you are lucky enough to find people who want to be around you because you know about weird things . . . those are friends."

"Yeah! Duh, Spaulding," Lucy said, giving him a gentler smack to the arm. "I'll even call you Boat now if you want."

He gave her a crooked smile, rubbing his arm. "Nah. I guess I kind of got to liking Spaulding."

Mr. Radzinsky clapped his hands together briskly. "There now, you see? All's well. And I'll be back before you know it. Just . . . do make sure you stay away from the mines while I'm gone, won't you?" Mr. Radzinsky gave them both one last smile and turned back to the pit.

Spaulding blinked, and the ghost was gone.

"Are we going to do what he said and stay away, Spaulding?" Lucy asked. "Or do we have to try to figure out where that tunnel goes?"

"Absolutely not," Spaulding said. "I am officially retired from paranormal research. Maybe even regular research—that can get risky around here, too."

The sun sank below the clouds again, and the pond turned back to its usual shade of inky black. Spaulding and Lucy got back on the bike and set out for home.

They rode back to town in silence. Just as they passed the shopping center, a crowd of kids on bikes turned onto Main Street, headed straight toward them. As the group got closer, Spaulding recognized the cloud of Marietta's black hair.

And before he could think better of it, the words had already left his mouth: "You should be wearing your helmet, Marietta!" he called.

Marietta's eyes widened in horror.

Next to her, Katrina slammed on her brakes and skidded to a halt. She gave a hoot of laughter. "Oh my *God*, Mar," she said. "Isn't that just so sweet? Psycho Spaulding's *worried* about you!"

Spaulding stopped too, his cheeks burning as he clenched his fists around his handlebars. Why couldn't he ever, *ever* keep his mouth shut?

From her perch behind him, Lucy tapped his shoulder impatiently. "Come on, Spaulding! Just ignore them."

But before he could obey, Marietta spoke. "You know what, Katrina?"

Katrina glanced over, still smirking. "What?"

"Sometimes," Marietta took a deep breath and then slowly let it out. "Sometimes you should just. Shut. Up." She unclipped her bike helmet from her handlebars and jammed it down over her curls. Then she turned to Spaulding. "There," she said. "*That* makes up for it."

And then she rode off—not with Spaulding, but not with Katrina, either.

As Marietta disappeared around a corner, Katrina scowled

Katrina in Utter Defeat (prob. never to be seen again, so am recording here for posterity).

at Spaulding. "Unbelievable," she said. "You're *so* overpower-ingly lame that your lameness lames up everyone you come in contact with, and now you've ruined Marietta."

Spaulding just grinned.

When he got home, all was quiet except for the distant tapping of Aunt Gwen at her keyboard. Spaulding went straight to the kitchen to make a p.c.-and-j. But as he took out the sup-plies, the sound of typing stopped.

Aunt Gwendolyn came into the room. "Spaulding!"

He hid the chip bag behind his back. "Hi, Aunt Gwen. I was just—"

"Getting something to eat? Well, no need—I made you a snack."

Oh, great. Reheated stew? Oven-baked kale chips?

But his aunt held out a plate bearing a sandwich. "Two kinds of chips and three kinds of jelly." She winked. "I think you've earned it."

Acknowledgments

I wish I had unlimited pages for this! I grew up in such a caring community that I can't possibly thank everyone individually who has supported and encouraged me over the years. So, to the people of Plumas County: thank you for making our corner of the world a warm and generous place.

I owe thanks to so many artists. To name just a few: Allen Stenzel, Kris Patzlaff, Sarah Whorf, and Jim Moore. To Dianne Lipscomb: you're so much more than one of my art teachers! I've learned so much from you, not only about art, but also about how to be a stronger, bolder, braver person.

To wonderful librarians: Margaret Miles, Sharla Satterfield, and Sherry Kumler; and especially to Jeanette Brauner, who made the library a welcoming place for a shy homeschooled oddball. To my funny, smart, kind, endlessly inspiring library kids—Serena, Auggie, Tenaya, Lily, River, Hank, Adeline, Toby, Addy, Emmy, Kaleb, Levi, Maeve, Violet, Lucius, Sam, Marlin, Emily, Maddie, Kiah, Dylan, Kaitlynn, and so many others: I write for you guys. You give me hope for the future.

Thanks to the warm-hearted, witty, and frighteningly multi-talented Ellie Sipila. Many thanks to Stacey Graham. Thanks to Heather Kelly, Ardi Alspach, Sari Lampert Murray, and the whole team at Sterling. And I truly can't find the words

Acknowledgments

to properly express my gratitude to my brilliant, insightful, and kind editor, Christina Pulles. Christina, you made this book worlds better than I ever could have done alone.

To Colleen, whose generosity helped make this possible. To Rajinder, for advice, endless kindness, book chats, movie nights, and for raising my standards in chai tea. To Lil, for years of vicarious thrills.

To Jenn, the very definition of a BFF. Thank you for never getting tired of me, even when I was being a know-it-all, or bossy, or painfully dorky (a total Spaulding, in other words).

To my mom and dad. Thank you for a million things, but to keep it book-related: thanks for introducing me to all the books that would remain my lifelong favorites. For letting me spend entire days reading. For letting me prop my books up in front of my plate at dinner so I didn't have to stop reading even to eat or, you know, talk or anything dumb like that. For also letting me watch waaay too much TV. (I still say I was learning story structure and comedic timing.)

And, of course, to Billy. For pep talks whenever I'm discouraged, for talking out plot points with me endlessly, for making dinners so I could work (even when it didn't really look like work), and then cleaning up dinner too, even though it wasn't your turn.

Finally, to everyone who read this book: thank you so much for spending some time in Thedgeroot with me! I hope we can do it again soon.